The War on Magic

Kade Taylor

iUniverse®

THE WAR ON MAGIC

iUniverse books may be ordered through booksellers or by contacting:

iUniverse
1663 Liberty Drive
Bloomington, IN 47403
www.iuniverse.com
844-349-9409

ISBN: 978-1-6632-5144-2 (sc)
ISBN: 978-1-6632-5145-9 (e)

Library of Congress Control Number: 2023904722

Print information available on the last page.

iUniverse rev. date: 03/10/2023

Dedications

To my family, who always believe in me.
To all those who inspire my work.
To my Father, who makes sense of the things
even I have trouble explaining.

Chapter 1

"I never found anything on an Arnold Lewis from what we know about Clemence. But I looked through the King's Royal guard, and among them, the name 'Dantalion' came up. I looked it up, and…"

The sun was at its peak, but obscured by the Gray clouds that covered the sky. Trees that stood like giants waved gently in the breeze and went on for miles all around, and the town of Goldberg observed noon on another Winter day.

Children ran around the playground in the school, and parents droned on with their work, be it at the local grocery store, one of the few convenience stores around, or any of the other businesses in the town.

In one neighborhood of Goldberg, an older white sedan pulled into the driveway, and a taller man wearing a blue superhero shirt and jeans stepped out after parking it. His hair was like a brown nest upon his head as he entered the small trailer house that sat behind the driveway.

As he entered, he was greeted by 2 large labradors, both a light brown and white mixture.

"Hey bu-buddy," he cooed to one of the large canines,

"Where's Albert? Go get him!" He said, excitement in his voice to emit the same level of excitement from the dogs. They both ran down the hallway to the man's right, past 2 doors and into a third at the end of the hall, bursting the door open and jumping on the bed where Albert was just about to sleep.

Albert Barrett winced as he felt the dogs bounce and trample him, not knowing that they were disturbing him in any way as they happily trotted all over his back and legs. His crystal blue eyes peeked through his long, dark hair.

Albert twisted himself and sat up, huffing as he looked to the doorway.

"Clay, you dick! I told you to stop riling them up like that!"

Clay walked into the room, rolling and cracking his neck as he leaned on the doorway.

"Not my fault, they just like me too much," Clay responded as Albert got out of bed, the dogs quickly becoming bored and leaving the room to explore the house, which they had explored countless times before.

"How was work?" Albert asked. His dark brown hair fell over his face and all around his head, hanging down near his shoulders in the back and just past his jawline closer to the front.

"Not bad, same old same old," Clay answered.

"You finish your paperwork for the military?" He asked, following Albert as the both of them walked back down the hall towards the living room.

"Yeah, I finished it, sent it in, all that. Now I'm just waiting for confirmation so I can ship out," Albert said, sitting on the couch and stretching.

"Does mom know?" Clay asked, sitting on the recliner just to the right of the couch, facing the television mounted to the wall and grabbing the remote.

"Nah, but I finished it right before dad went to work," Albert said as Clay turned on the TV, a news report halfway through its course.

"This is the fifth sighting of the magic-user group 'the Red Hand' this year in the nation of Tarren, and the twenty-first worldwide since the beginning of the year, a record high. While most of the Magic Users were said to be killed within Tarren, a number still remain in hiding, and as they group together, remain a threat to the Tarren people," Said the news reporter.

"Oh yeah, scary Houdini's are gonna come blow our door open and get us all," Clay said. Albert was laughing along with him.

"Yeah, like there could be that many left in the country, let alone a number of them who're actually evil or something," Albert said.

"Thankfully, Chancellor Jackson Ambrose has agreed to strengthen the budget of the magic Suppression Force, in an attempt to subdue any and all signs of Magic Users across Tarren, and a new plan to expand military forces to help combat Magic Users in nearby nations such as Brakata or Virtuin. The MSF has said in an interview they plan on establishing outposts throughout Tarren to better combat the threats that have surfaced," The news reporter said. A tall, white man in a suit with blonde hair tied back in a ponytail stood at a podium, speaking towards the camera that the TV broadcasted. His eyes were a warm yellow color, like molten gold within his irises.

"We believe that these heinous sightings have been happening around the many geysers in Tarren and Brakata. We are currently working with Brakata's internal affairs brigade to establish a way to efficiently stop these Magic Users from bringing any more harm to the people of our nations," He said.

"What year did we take the world back again?" Albert looked at his phone, typing away as Clay looked over.

"Well, the Second Great War ended in '45, so I'm guessing sometime around then. Why?" Clay said while Albert continued typing.

"Just wondering how long it's been. You'd think after what, 75 years? That they'd kill the last of them off so nobody has to worry about it," Albert said.

"Maybe they already did and this is just some scare tactic by the government to keep us under their thumb?" Clay shrugged.

"Well, for most people, it does the trick. Seems like everyone around here is always on edge whenever those people are mentioned," Albert said.

"People? That's awfully generous…" Clay said, rolling his eyes and channel flipping again.

It was a brief while before Albert got a call from his mother, asking him to bring her an extra jacket. The clouds in the sky had made what was to be a cold winter day even colder, though not enough to bring about snow. The most they had gotten was a layer of frost that morning as the dew lightly froze to the plants it rested on.

As Albert arrived at the local Market Store, a grocery store that had been open almost as long as the town had existed, he got out of the same Sedan that Clay had used to get home earlier, grabbing a thick brown jacket that belonged to his mother out of the backseat and walking inside.

In the store, a single shelf on the wall and one in the open area of the floor led Albert to the right, towards the produce section, where his mother was stocking bags of whole spinach in a red apron, black hat, a black shirt and khakis, with a pair of clear gloves over her hands.

His mother was a shorter woman, contrary to both he and his brother, who must have inherited their heights from her father since both her and her husband, the father of the two, stand no taller than 5'7" while both boys were well over 6ft.

"Damn, it's almost as cold in here as it is outside," He said as he approached his mother, putting out his arm that held her jacket.

"Yeah, why do you think I needed the extra jacket?" She chuckled as she took it, sliding her arms into the sleeves. She pulled her dyed black hair up through the collar of the jacket, letting it flow down to just above the small of her back.

"Don't you think that wearing gloves but having your hair down is a bit redundant?" Albert asked.

"Hey, you know how my scalp is. Hair ties hurt, and I'm not about to wear a hair net. Half the town would be laughing at me before I left work," She said, still stocking the cold spinach.

"If you say so," He half-rolled his eyes and turned away from her before she looked up and stopped him.

"Hey, did you send in that paperwork?" She asked, shaking her outstretched hand at him.

"Yes, I sent it in, I'm just waiting for a shipping date," He said, turning back to her slowly, half wincing in preparation for her response.

"I don't know what in the world makes you want to go out there and fight like that, all that violence, death, and all those Magic Users people," she began. "I wouldn't even let Rick go in, simply cause we were about to have Clay,"

"Hey, you know those guys are nearly wiped out. I'm not worried about them, I just want a way to protect myself and pay for an education," He said.

"There's plenty of ways to pay off your school than going and killing for a living," She said, raising her eyebrows and puffing her lips with sass.

"Well, unless the entire school board is gay, I don't think I can get in the way you did,"

The woman looked at him, her brow furrowed and her mouth agape for just a moment.

"If I wasn't afraid I'd lose my job I would whip your ass right here and now, you listen to me little boy I will take you out of this world the same way I brought you into it!" She raised her voice as she spoke at him.

"You'll what?! How do you mean?!" He said, backing up with a half disgusted look on his face. The woman looked at the floor for a second, a blank stare as she processed the words that came out of her mouth.

"Oh, you nasty little shit, you know what I meant!" She said, grabbing an orange and throwing it, nearly missing his head and letting the orange roll down the aisle behind him.

"Now get outta here before you get me in trouble," She said, shaking her head and walking towards the fruit she had displaced while Albert moved to leave the section.

"Hold on, I'm gonna pick up a drink. You want anything?" He asked as he walked towards the registers and the small coolers beside them.

The military had been on Albert's mind for weeks now, thinking about where he'd be stationed, what job he would take, the money and everything else that came with it, but after 2 people mentioned them, his mind wandered while he laid in bed that night, thinking about the Magic Users.

Grabbing his phone, he pulled up his web browser and typed away.

"Why are there still Magic Users?"

The first result, an official anatomy website, said "Magic Users' abilities are hereditary. If a Magic Users has a child, that child will inherit the parent's ability,"

Albert's brow furrowed as he thought about the article.

"What happens when two Magic Users have a child?"

Just before he hit enter on the search bar, Clay burst into the room.

"Hey!" He said, staring at Albert from the doorway after the attempt to scare him.

Albert looked up, sitting up in his bed, a bored expression on his face.

"What?" He blankly asked.

"You need to go pick up mom from the store. Dad got caught in traffic or something," Clay said.

"Traffic? There's barely 1,000 people in this town," Albert replied.

"I dunno, he just said there was something going on outside town. He's stuck in a line of cars," Clay said.

"Ugh… why can't you? You're already up," Albert said.

"Cause it's your car," Clay said.

"Ugh, it's only my car when you don't wanna do something," Albert said, getting up and putting on his shoes.

--------- ✦ ◆ ✦ ◆ ✦ ---------

Albert got into his car and drove the same 10 blocks, give or take, to the grocery store, but on approach, he noticed a plume of smoke begin to rise from the area. He watched it as he made the turn towards the store, seeing the smoke flowing from the vents and roof of the building. Flames were bursting out the windows, yet the entryway seemed like it wasn't too covered by the raging fire.

Albert got out of the car, leaving it parked in the middle of the parking lot as he ran to the doorway, and seeing his mother near the produce, he ran inside to help her.

"Albert, you need to leave, now," She said as he helped her up.

"What are you talking about? Come on, we need to-"

Before Albert could finish his sentence, he saw a man standing near the doorway, a bored expression on his face. The man's black hair matched his clothes, a black jumpsuit that hugged his thin form.

"Hey, what are you doing?" He called to him, the man turning to face them, flames already engulfing half his face.

"Oh, missed a couple," He said, walking towards the two. His right hand erupted into flames without warning, and as he brought it up, Albert's mother pushed him aside, both of them falling away from each other just as a plume of flames soared towards them, missing and hitting the shelving behind them.

The shelf tipped one way, then the other, sending boxes and cans of food falling all over the tile floor below, many of them now in flames, the cardboard and paper burning away as Albert looked up at what he now realized was a Magic-User.

His mother grabbed a knife from one of the burnt cutlery kits nearby, pulling it out and running at the man, screaming as he looked up, his eyes widening as he grabbed her arm with both hands. She bore down with both arms, slowly bringing the knife down as she fought against his grasp. The attacker's hands glowed red, and soon smoke began rising from the spots he held the woman's arms, yet her screams in pain didn't stop her from pushing the knife further towards him, the blade slowly pushing past his jumpsuit and drawing blood in his stomach before she was shoulder tackled to the side, knocked to the ground by someone else.

Albert and his mother both looked up at the one who had knocked her away from their assailant. The thing they saw hardly even seemed human…

A beast on two legs. Fur over his body, the snout of a dog and the claws of a bear… the beast stood almost 7 feet tall, towering above everyone else there. He wore another jumpsuit, this one straining to cover his form without tearing.

"Lupos… thanks," The Fire user said, backing up to nurse his wounds.

The beast, Lupos, walked forward towards the mother as she stood, still holding the blade, its tip now crimson with the blood of the pyromaniac she had attacked. But as she lunged at Lupos, the blade fell from her hands with one blow from its massive hand, and a second strike sent its claws deep into her stomach, pushing at the skin of her back for an exit that would barely refuse.

Albert watched his mother's eyes widen as she let out all the air in her lungs, realization crossing her face that she had just been stabbed, not with a blade, but with the claws of a Magic-User.

The beast dropped the woman, letting her blood flow over the tile as both he and the pyromaniac looked at Albert.

"Let me take care of this one," The black-haired man said, holding his wound and walking towards Albert.

"Such a weak race… why'd we ever let you have this world?" He asked, his hand igniting once more as he raised it towards Albert, who was frozen with fear, unable to get to his feet and only sat, hands behind him, staring into the eyes of the man about to kill him…

"Vin!" Lupos yelled.

Before the man fired, his arm was grabbed, and Albert looked up to see his father.

Albert's dad head-butted the Fire user, grasping his arm. The flames both on Vin's hands and around his face and neck dissipated quickly as the Father drove his knee into the man's gut, Lupos only now realizing what was happening and moving to help the pyromaniac.

"Rick…" Albert's mother whispered from the ground.

Albert's Father pushed Vin aside and let him hold his stomach on the ground as he faced the approaching beast. Rick reached out, grabbing his arm as he went to stab him the same way he had done with Albert's mother, but as his hand made contact, it was not the claws that hit him, but the fingers of the man, no longer a beast.

Lupos looked at his hand before looking up at Rick, who retaliated with a straight punch to his jaw, sending him to the side near Vin.

Albert slowly stood and looked over at Rick, who was kneeling down beside his mother.

"Erica…" Rick could only say, holding his hand over her wound.

The woman silently looked up at Rick, then at Albert as he walked over. She looked to Rick again, narrowing her tired eyes just a bit.

"Rick… keep them… away… from this…" Erica said.

Rick paused, looking back as both of the Magic Users were slowly starting to regain their composure.

Setting Erica down, he kissed her forehead as she closed her eyes.

"We need to go, now. These two aren't the only Magic Users in town. I'm sorry… there's nothing we can do for your mother," He said. That's when Albert noticed the tears in his eyes… he had never cried before, from what Albert had seen, and he didn't want to start now. Albert could only imagine how hard it was for his father to leave her… but it hurt just as bad for him, too.

"Okay… okay. Where are we going?"

There was Chaos throughout the town, Magic Users wiping out both civilians and police in the area. The Magic Users were working together to protect each other while subsequently wiping out their enemies. Dozens of police and hundreds of innocent people were being slaughtered by the homicidal group of Magic Users while Albert and his dad left the grocery store.

The two attackers rose as they heard emergency sirens in the distance.

"Those aren't local forces…" one of them said as he turned back into the beast, looking at the pyromaniac .

"Vale, we need to pull everyone out. We lose too many here, we might not get a second run," He said, picking up the man, Vale, and dusting him off.

"Alright, alright, I get it…" he said, looking at his hands as the fire began to return to them.

"What was that…?"

The two left the store, moving to round up the rest of the Magic Users and exit the town.

✦◆◆◆✦

"What's going on?"

Clay was asking questions the second his dad and Albert came in without his mother.

While it took a while to explain to Clay what had happened, Albert and his father both started packing up their things.

"So, mom told us she'd meet us outside of town. We'll head out once we have our clothes packed," Albert explained to Clay.

"As long as they didn't bring any of the Wild Ones with them, we should be able to get out of town easily," Albert's father said, bringing his suitcase into the living room.

Albert paused as he brought his own in, Clay still packing his things up.

"Wild Ones?" He asked, Rick holding his forehead.

"It's hard to explain. When two people who have tapped into their magic potential have a child, it… well, the child's mind isn't able to process the power alone. Depending on the power, they go insane, tend to become feral. Something about the serum in their blood being too much for their brain to process,"

Albert's brow furrowed as he thought.

"Serum? Dad, what are you talking about? What do you mean,' depending on the power?'" Albert asked, checking his phone as news stories about the attack on Goldberg began to surface already.

"Well, someone who has 2 healing powers will be fine for a long time, since-" He said, looking outside at the front yard. Albert's father froze mid-sentence as he stared outside, Albert following his eyes to see a figure outside. It's eyes were those of a broken man, circles under them as they stared at the ground. One of his arms was deformed, bulged out in spots and thinner in others, with his hand the shape of a sort of blade, with what would have been his fingernails making up the edge and tip of the blade.

"Albert, get Clay, and get my gun," Rick said, walking outside and down the steps that led to the porch, seeing the eyes of the man dart up to meet his own.

"Jason…" the man groaned, walking towards him. Rick balled up his fists, raising them as the man lunged forward, going for a stab into his stomach.

Rick sidestepped the attack and grabbed where the man's wrist would have been, pulling him forward and wrapping his arm around the attacker's neck.

The man swung around as Albert and Clay came outside, Albert holding his father's old 1911.

"Take the shot!" Rick yelled, keeping his grip on the monstrous human as Albert aimed, his hands shaking as he tried to aim.

"Albert, kill it! Now!" He yelled at Albert as he tried to aim, hesitation holding him back before he finally closed his eyes and fired.

The bullet flew past the two into a nearby tree behind them.

"Where is… Jason?" The wild one asked.

The attacker drove his blade hand into the foot of Rick, forcing him to let go. He then turned and drove his blade forward, stabbing through Rick's stomach and picking him up in the air.

Albert stared in horror as his father was stabbed, blood pouring down the monster's arm. Albert looked his father in the eyes, Rick looking back at him.

"Take the… damn… shot," He said with as much air as he could.

Albert looked at the creature… it didn't even seem like a human being anymore. Its arm, its ravenous behavior… it was an animal. A dangerous animal.

Albert took aim again, steadying his hand before he fired.

The wild one fell, dropping Rick as Albert fired again, and again, and again. He kept firing until the gun was empty, pulling the trigger several more times and making the weapon harmlessly click in response.

Clay ran to his father, Flipping Rick over and holding him in his arms.

"Dad… no…" he said, tears forming around his eyes. Albert turned to Clay and his dad as he dropped the gun, falling to his knees a moment after.

"Find… Ichabod…" Rick whispered to Clay. Clay looked at him, his eyes widening a moment as Rick closed his eyes, his chest no longer moving with his breaths.

"Who…?" Clay asked, but realized right after what happened. He pressed his head against his father's chest, shaking as Albert stood, looking over the dead creature before him.

"They took them both…" he whispered to himself, looking down at the gun, then at Clay. He picked up the weapon, took the magazine out and went back inside.

"Clay, get the car ready," He said, entering the house.

❖ ✦ ❖ ✦ ❖

By the time Albert came back outside, the car was loaded up and started, and Clay was outside digging in the front yard, a sheet from their bed laid over Rick. Albert had a holster for the gun now, with 2 extra magazines on his belt as well, both of them fully loaded.

Albert looked at Clay as he walked towards the car, stopping as he saw him digging the hole.

"What are you doing?" He asked, putting his hands in his pockets and walking towards him slowly.

"Giving our father…" Clay said as he stabbed the shovel into the ground again.

"A proper burial…"

Albert sighed, looking down at the sheet.

"After all this is over, they'll give him one anyway. We have work to do,"

Clay looked up, panting as he pushed the shovel into the grass beside him.

"Work? Doing what? There's nothing else we can do!" He yelled, Albert silently locking eyes with him.

"If this thing was here, I'm sure there's more nearby. We need to get rid of them," He said, walking to the car.

"The hell are you gonna do?! Just gonna go Gun-Ho into a bunch of Magic Users so they'll make mince meat of you?!" Clay yelled, walking towards the car. Albert looked back at him, his brow furrowing.

"I'm not going to let them do to other families what they just did to us!" He yelled back, Clay stopping in his tracks, both of them staring into each others' eyes for a moment.

"Albert… you're going to get yourself killed," Clay said flatly. Albert looked at his father's body, the sheet over him now stained with a large blood spot.

"Don't go out there. I'm sure the MSF are hearing about this now," Clay said, lowering his voice to try and calm Albert down.

Albert looked down, first at the gun on his hip, then at his hand.

"If you want to go after these things, you should. But doing it with the government, which equips you to deal with them, is much better than just going out like some Vigilante who thinks he can take on the world with a gun from the forties!" Clay yelled again, this time out of his own anger.

Albert nodded, shutting the car door and leaning on the side, putting his face in his hands as he slid down to sit in front of one of the tires. Clay ran over and pulled him into a hug, burying Albert's head in his shoulder as both of them teared up again.

"Let's just go… we need to meet mom," Clay said. Albert stared at the ground, before sighing, giving a nod.

"The Red Hand have really outdone themselves this time,"

A Humvee filled with soldiers kitted out with Kevlar vests, assault rifles and ballistic masks rolled down the road as part of a convoy of about 10, accompanied by 2 helicopters, each with a man with a rifle sitting on the sides for recon.

"Think they'll bring in Titan squad?" One of the soldiers asked.

"Nah, not unless they think there's someone here who we can't handle,"

"What, you mean there's a Magic User that bullpup here couldn't take?"

The soldiers laughed at one of their own, who had a bullpup rifle rather than the M16's that most of them held.

"Hey, don't down talk the Bullpup. It's not traditional, but it gets the job done. Plus, me and this rifle are about to be promoted, and given command over a squad, so you might want to show a little respect," He replied.

The Humvees entered Goldberg, splitting off to sweep the streets as 2 of them drove into the parking lot of the grocery store. The soldiers moved out from the Humvees, weapons raised as they moved to the entrance, one of them kneeling to see a woman on the ground with a stab wound through her abdomen.

"Claws. Lupos was through here. Which means…" one of the soldiers said, standing as Bullpup looked around, seeing the cans and boxes on the floor from the shelf tipping.

"Vale was here, too. Call in Titan Squad," The squad commander said, looking down the aisles, then observing the claw marks on the ground.

"We need to do a full sweep. Put it on the radio that Vale is here somewhere. We don't want to capture, we just want to try following him back to the Red Hand's Rat-hole," Bullpup spoke as he walked back, past his squad to the Humvees.

"Another thing. There was a scuffle here. I want that body identified. Anyone connected to that person, send me any information we have on them,"

Chapter 2

*"Clay, Albert and Vincent took the other truck, opening the truck
with the same crowbar that Vincent made last time. Inside the
truck, they heard a struggling from the bottom of the stretchers,
and began unloading the stretchers to make their way to the
source. It was just a minute before Lupos ran over to them,"*

In the year 1912, a nation by the name of "Clemence" laid siege to the world. With an army of people with superhuman abilities, Clemence conquered a quarter of the world in less than two months. In 1916, The Great War originally was to decide the fate of the world, when three nations from across the sea declared war on Clemence to stop their advance. However, 2 years after the war started, the Nations failed, and for 20 years, Clemence sat unopposed. Until these three nations, armed with new technologies and weaponry, attacked Clemence, and in a shocking turn of events, Clemence's high-ranked military and political figures disappeared, leaving their army disorganized and their people ungoverned. The Nations who fought back their army installed 4 new nations out of the land Clemence held. Tarren, in the North, Brakata, to the south, Boleyn, to the East, and Virtuin, on the NorthWestern Islands. The method of creating Magic Users died as Clemence did, with nobody figuring out why or how Magic Users came to be.

Clay and Albert were left to pick up the pieces of their house, their inheritance from their parents' life insurance covering the funeral costs and burials for both of their parents and leaving their house to the both of them. It wasn't long after the death of both of their parents that Clay and Albert both joined the military. Clay never saw his mother again, simply assuming one of the Magic Users got her on her way out.

7 Months Later

"Barrett C! Get moving!"

Technical Sergeant Oroc shouted as the recruits all ran with rifles and backpacks through the grassy plains within their training ground, towards a heavily wooded area up ahead.

Sergeant Oroc, the instructor for Clay and Albert's group, was a taller man, standing at a rigid 6'4". His tanned skin and dark hair made most trainees unaware of his ethnicity, but none ever asked him about such. His brown eyes were always filled with intensity, and his voice was the personification of urgency.

"Hurry up! Hurry up! HURRY UP!" Sergeant Oroc yelled. Clay struggled to keep his legs moving, but pressed on, just barely keeping up with the rest of the group. However, as he started to fall back, another trainee slowed down and grabbed him underneath the arm, lifting him slightly so the weight on his legs was lessened, letting him catch up.

The trainee was just a bit taller than Clay, but had double the muscles. He was tanned, with deep brown eyes and a voice as deep as the Mariana Trench.

"Parks... thanks," Clay said. This wasn't the first time since they began boot camp that Parks had helped him.

As they ran, Clay remembered some of the hand-to-hand combat training sessions they had, where Parks was constantly giving him pointers on how to defend against attackers.

"Remember, when you're up against an aggressive attacker, the trick is to always use their momentum against them. If they lunge forward, sidestep and push them further forward. Especially if they're stronger than you, don't try to push them back," Parks said. He began an attack, swinging with his left at Clay, who ducked under and grabbed his wrist, pulling him forward and putting his free elbow into Parks' shoulder blade, forcing him to the ground.

"Good…" Parks said as Clay let him go and helped him up.

Back to the present, Albert remained within the middle, keeping his head down as he moved forward at a brisk pace, his breathing still steady but a bit labored with the weight on him.

"At this rate, some wild Magic-User is gonna rip your head off at first sight! Hurry up!" The instructor yelled, Clay ducking his head down and pushing forward, gradually making his way through the crowd until he was nearly at the middle. Sergeant Oroc nodded as he jogged alongside them, only a water bottle in his hand.

"Cross that first tree, then get into formation!" The instructor yelled as he stopped, watching his trainees pass the tree and immediately rush to their position, 4 men across and 8 rows, 32 men in the class. The instructor stepped forward in front of them, waving forward as a group of 2 men and 1 woman came forward.

The first man was a slender, blonde-haired man, in his thirties. His hair was cut with the sides faded and his top a bit longer, though not long enough to break the regulation. The second was a bald African man, taller and built a bit more than the first, roughly in his mid-thirties. The third was a short but firmly built woman, in her early twenties, with Aviators over her eyes and jet-black hair tied up in a bun. They were all in military uniform, the spots designated for their ranks to be attached replaced with an insignia of a sword aimed upwards, the center of the cross guard gleaming in the design.

"Trainees. This is Sergeants Vincent Johnson, Julie Alvarez, and Adam Vander Esch, of Titan Squad. They're here to Evaluate you while you go on your first assignment,"

The trainees all seemed off-put by the news, everyone except Clay, Albert, and a select few others.

"Hey! I don't wanna hear a single complaint about it! I don't care what they can or can't do, they are your superiors and you will treat them with the same damn respect you treat any other sergeant of this army, do you understand me?!" Instructor Oroc yelled at the formation, triggering a resounding "Yes, Sir!" From them all.

The trainees watched as a group of 7 black Humvees approached, the instructor not flinching as they parked beside the group.

"Alright, three to a truck! There'll be 2 in the back of the front truck, and I'll be riding in that one. Barrett C, Matthews, Prescott, you're in the back!"

Instructor Oroc went down the row of trucks, skipping the back one for Titan Squad to ride in. He continued until he reached the front truck.

"Parks, Barrett A, you're in with me," He said, pointing to the truck for them to get in before the instructor got in the front seat. The convoy of Humvees moved out, heading south.

Albert looked over at Parks, a taller trainee, with tanned skin and what little hair he had extremely dark. Albert himself had his hair cut as well, in uniform with the rest of the trainees, whose hair was all cut almost down to bare skin.

Sergeant Oroc got over the radio to the rest of the trucks, talking to the trainees as the drivers silently moved the Humvees along.

"This assignment is simple. Part of you will be on patrol, part of you will be security, and the rest will start on a break period. You will take shifts doing each task for the next 3 days. Once you complete this assignment, you'll be getting ready and practicing for the graduation ceremony. In other words, this is it. Don't act stupid just because you're not on the training grounds for the next couple of days,"

Albert stared at his boots, thinking as the instructor put the radio back.

"This is it…" Parks quietly said to Albert, "Just one assignment and we're qualified soldiers,"

Albert looked up to the other trainee, Parks' glasses as thick as their Humvee's ballistic glass windows.

Albert looked back down at the floor mats of the Humvee, clutching his currently unloaded assault rifle to his chest.

"Yeah… just one assignment,"

The Humvees pulled up on the edge of the Capital of Tarren, Rotun. The city was massive, with skyscrapers on the inside of the city reaching high into the air. Around the suburbs of Rotun were fields of geysers, all slowly pumping white and grey smoke into the atmosphere.

There sat a checkpoint to get into town, with guards standing on both sides of the road checking people's IDs as they entered and exited.

"Bring out your military ID; Hand it up front," Instructor Oroc said to Albert and Parks. Upon command, the both of them reached down their collars to the lanyards around their necks, pulling them out and picking their Military ID's from them for the instructor, who brought out his own as well along with the driver.

Once they had been given their ID's back and were let through, each of the Humvees stopped at a military compound near the edge of town. The trainees all got out of their transports, the instructor getting out as well and looking over the group of men.

"Get in formation! Now!" He said, walking to the field of grass as the trainees followed and got into formation in front of him as quickly as they could.

"Good. Now, before I explain the assignment, remember three things. One! Look out for your fellow man. Hold them accountable, but lift them up along with you. Trying to act alone doesn't cut it here. Two! Cover your asses. Do not have one person on a guard shift, just in case one of them falls asleep during duty. Three! Remember your codes. Red for Fire, Blue for Rain, and if you, by some ungodly circumstance, find a Magic User, signal a code Black at your location and pull back. Let the experienced men handle it," Sergeant Oroc told the class, his voice in a more down-to-earth tone.

"Do I make myself clear?" He asked.

"Yes, Sir!" Yelled the trainees, all of them with enthusiasm.

"Good. Make me proud, I've done my best to raise you all to be great soldiers. Don't let me down, and don't let yourselves down," He said.

"Yes, sir!" They replied.

"Alright! Then here's your assignment. Each one of you will be given a number," The instructor said. He went down the line, each trainee getting a number from one to three. Albert and Clay both ended up being number 3, while Parks was given 1.

"Group one! You are on patrol duty. You will be assigned to watch the wall on the outside of town, about a quarter-mile that way," He said, pointing to the other side of the field.

"Group two, you are on rest period. Go get some sleep in the barracks we have prepared for you, you're gonna need as much as you can get. This is to be considered a deployment, so you're dismissed. Get up there," The instructor commanded. Immediately, the men who drew number two moved into the compound and up the stairs within.

"Group three! You're on security detail. I want each of you posted on a different part of the compound, and 2 men patrolling the halls and stairs at all times. You'll get your rest period next, in six hours. Group one, set your watches for six hours, then head back to the compound, group two will take your place and you'll be on Security detail," The instructor said,

"For the next 3 days, you will all keep to the schedule given, or if you decide to change the time of shift changes, coordinate with your Dorm Chief, Parks. Check your radios, and keep the other groups and yourself accountable for everything here. Your radios should all be tuned to frequency 4, which is designated for you. Do not turn frequencies. If we need to tell you something, we'll turn to your's. Understood?"

The trainees all gave a resounding "Yes, sir!" And the instructor nodded before stepping back into the Humvee, six of the seven moving out, while Titan Squad's transport stayed where it was, the passengers remaining inside for the moment.

It was almost time for the shift change when Albert and Clay met up near the front door of the barracks after a brief patrol around the first floor.

"You know what they say, a boring job is a good one when we're in here," Clay said, attaching his rifle to the clip on his vest as he leaned on the wall beside the door, Albert doing the same but keeping his weight on his feet as he hung his arms on his collar, his fingers holding the vest as his arms relaxed.

"I did some research on the Magic User attacks before we shipped out. Apparently most of the attacks, including the one on Goldberg, were on towns that were close to the Geysers around the country. Apparently there's a pretty big geyser around here somewhere," Albert said, looking down the hall as his radio crackled, one of the others in their group checking in.

"All clear on the South side, over," The voice called over.

"All clear front door, over," Albert replied, before looking back to Clay.

"I don't know what it is about those geysers. Maybe they have some weird effect on people?" Albert said. Clay was tugging on his gloves to make sure they fit tightly around his wrists without cutting off his circulation. The gloves had open backs, but completely covered the palms and fingers besides the knuckles, Albert wearing the same glove on one hand while the other was bare.

"Don't you think if they did, that the government would warn people? Especially after Goldberg, I doubt they'd want to let their own population turn into Magic Users. Plus, there's no connection besides the attacks being near them. Geysers are everywhere; that may not be anything," Clay shrugged, keeping his foot stance wide but still leaning on the wall.

"Well, considering magic is a genetic thing after Clemence's soldiers got it, I doubt there would really be anymore of those things around these days. You would think-" Albert began.

"I know, I know, you've said this before. I don't know where they're coming from or how they're popping up. All I know is I hope we don't have to deal with them very much," Clay interrupted.

"I hope we do… after what happened back home… I'm gonna kill them all. Every last one…" Albert replied.

Before either of them could continue the conversation, a strange feeling washed over them both. A sense of Deja Vu, a very slight dizziness that made them both look at one another, concerned. They both recognized that the other had felt it, but before they could address the feeling, Clay looked down at his radio, an unfamiliar voice coming over.

"Trainees, turn to frequency 6,"

Clay grabbed his radio, raising an eyebrow as Albert did the same, looking over the device.

"Turn to six? I thought we were told not to change frequency," Clay said, looking to Albert.

"Instructor Oroc said that they would turn to our frequency if they needed us. Obviously that's what they just did," Albert said sarcastically before turning his frequency, Clay doing the same right after.

"-Just outside the main gates. We're unsure of a target but they've neutralized our security at the SouthEast gate and they're moving West to-" a voice cut out from the radios, the two brothers looking at each other for a moment before Albert pulled out a map of the base, with one of their compound on the other side.

"The SouthEast gate, that's not far from here," Clay said, looking at the map over his shoulder.

"All units, this is Command point Bravo. We need any available units to the South region and SouthEast gate. This is Code Black, repeat, Code Black. Tangos are a Caucasian male, blue hair, dressed in black civies, and a male dressed in metal armor. Engage with caution, lethal force authorized,"

"A white guy in civvies, taking out security forces?" Albert and Clay were both frozen in place, Albert looking at the ground a moment.

"Magic Users…"

Albert tucked the map away, getting on his radio.

"Command Point Bravo, this is Trainee Barrett. En route to intercept," He said, Clay watching him and running after.

"Hey! You heard what Instructor Oroc said! We're supposed to pull back and let the experienced soldiers handle them!" Clay yelled, walking alongside Albert while trying to talk him down.

"Albert! Why are you so insistent on getting yourself killed?!" Clay asked, Albert still moving through the field to the main road nearby.

"Albert, listen to me! What makes you want to jump into this fight?!"

Albert finally stopped, looking Clay in the eyes and taking a step towards him, making Clay back up a bit.

"These things took everything from us! First, our mother by those psychos in town, then our father from that thing in our yard! You didn't watch the life fade from both of them. You didn't watch them both get stabbed! If you saw them die the same way I did, you would want to kill them all the same way I do!" Albert yelled at Clay, causing his head to spin slightly as he backed up more.

"Trainee, this is not your channel. Return to your post and turn back to your designated frequency," The woman on the radio said, Albert's brow furrowing as he looked back at it.

"Turn back? We were asked to turn to-"

Albert looked up and froze, Clay already nearly in shock as the two of them stared at two men in front of them, one of them dressed in all black, with a Kevlar vest and a pistol in his hand, the other dressed in some sort of medieval-looking armor with a short sword on his hip, kept in a scabbard clipped to him.

"These look like trainees… guess we're headed in the right direction," The man dressed in black said, looking to the armor-clad Magic User beside him.

"Exitium, mind disarming them?" He said, the armor-clad man nodding and outstretching his hand. A red aura surrounded his hand as he made a fist, pulling his arm back and causing the rifles on the brothers' chests to fly towards him.

"Thanks. That should make this easier," The other man said, walking over the rifles and looking the two trainees over.

"I should ask you before we do anything here, do you two know who the Magic Users are in your class? We came looking for them," The man said to the two, who only looked at each other both in shock and concern.

"Heh, guess not. I'm Lance, by the way, in case you wanted to know the name of your killer,"

Albert looked back at Lance, then at his rifle and Exitium.

"Lance…" Clay said, slowly raising his hands to his shoulders.

"Look, I don't know of any Magic Users in our class. But you don't have to-"

Before Clay could finish his sentence, Albert pulled his pistol from his holster, aiming and firing in only a second. Lance flinched, jumping backwards, while Exitium already had his arm up, the same red aura around his hand holding the bullet back while at the same time freezing Albert's arms in place.

"Damnit… thanks, E," Lance said as Exitium walked forward towards Albert, Lance stepping back as the armored man raised his fist up. Albert's arms spread apart immediately at Exitium's gesture. Albert winced, grinding his teeth as his arms were pulled away from his body, straining his muscles to keep them attached to his shoulders.

"Stop!" Clay yelled, running at Exitium. Lance put out his arm, a blue and white aura around his hand as he fired a wave of frost from it. Ice began to form around Clay's legs as he grabbed Exitium's arm, pulling it away. The armored man balled up one of his fists and swung at Clay, only for him to duck and without thinking, send a punch back.

The second Clay's knuckles slammed into Exitium's armor, he felt the muscles throughout his arm twitch, and the armored man fell to the ground. Albert fell to his knees, the grip that Exitium had on him letting go as the armor-clad attacker fell.

Lance's eyes widened as he saw this, looking to Albert as he pulled up his pistol again. Lance threw his arm up, a wall of Ice shooting up from the ground about 20 feet high just before Albert fired 3 times into it.

Clay looked over Exitium, his brow furrowing as he looked to his gloved hands, noticing his bare knuckles were red from the punch he threw and feeling his muscles all the way up his arm were slightly sore from the blow. He looked back down at the limp figure in front of him, kneeling down and grabbing one of the arms of it. The leather under armor kept the armor in place, but the arm felt... strangely light in his hand.

Albert moved around the wall of ice, noticing his and Clay's rifles were on the other side. Albert kept his pistol aimed as he moved forward, nearly reaching the wall before it grew, the sides being built on with more ice and extended around the two brothers until they were trapped within a circle of it.

Clay looked up at the top of the wall as Lance stood atop it, one of their rifles in his hand.

"That answers that question," Lance said, Albert seeing him and aiming up at him. Lance barely threw a barrier of ice up before 3 more shots were fired at the Magic User. Lance began to return fire, Albert and Clay both running right underneath Lance to block his view.

"We're sitting ducks in here!" Albert said, checking his pistol.

"Fuck, I'm out," He said, looking at Clay.

Clay pulled his pistol out, looking over the ice wall and taking out his knife, driving it into the ice and pulling on it, the knife not giving an inch when pulled in any direction but straight out the way it went in.

"I have an idea, but I'll need your pistol, and you'll need both of our knives," Clay said.

Clay jumped out from their cover and fired one of the pistols at Lance, causing him to pull back behind the ice barrier. Shot after shot, a few seconds apart, Clay fired 5 shots at the attacker above, finally stopping and only firing when he saw movement near the edge of the barrier. Lance stayed behind the barrier before the last two shots from Clay's pistol fired, Lance looked over.

"That's seven, dumbass!" He yelled before seeing Clay drop the pistol and pull a second from behind his back, originally Albert's. One shot hit his arm as Lance went back down, a second hitting the ice as Lance yelled in pain.

"Shit!" Lance yelled from the barrier, holding his arm. Clay watched the top of the wall, his eyes darting down every now and then as he kept Lance pinned behind his cover. Finally, he used his last bullet, Lance popping back up, a psychotic smile on his face.

"Alright, now it's time for you to die!" He yelled, before hearing Albert yell right beside him.

Lance looked over as Albert, with a knife in his hand, tackled Lance to the floor of the Ice wall. He and Lance fought over the rifle, Albert finally tossing it into the circle of ice for Clay. Albert grabbed Lance's throat with his bare hand. Albert felt a shock through his hand, a cold, like it was about to freeze right before him. But as he gripped the man's throat, he felt his body push back against the feeling, forcing it away.

Lance was struggling to do something, anything to escape Albert's grasp, realizing the aura around his hands was gone.

Albert raised his knife into the air, Lance reaching out and grabbing his wrist as Albert brought it down, the both of them struggling against the blade. Lance winced as his throat was squeezed, the life fading from him as the blade neared his stomach. Clay watched on, his eyes widening as he saw his brother trying to kill the man. He was frozen, not in a physical sense, but in fear of what was happening. A thousand thoughts raced through his head.

The guy's already beaten, he's stopped fighting back, but Albert is still attacking. Clay knew he'd have to kill or be killed if he wanted to survive, but this…

He has him nearly defenseless, but is still choosing to kill him…

But before Clay could do or say anything, he felt something grab his back and throw him forward. Clay slammed into the ice wall before falling to the ground; the wind knocked him out. Clay struggled to look up, staying on the ground but turning his head to see Exitium standing again, raising his arm and pulling both Lance and Albert down from the ice wall. Albert was dropped to the ground, Lance being set down just behind Exitium. Albert stood, gripping his knife and running at the armored man before being thrown backwards, his body slamming into the ice and cracking it. Albert fell, his eyes closing as he went limp on the ground just as Clay was, barely conscious.

"We've made enough of a mess here already. Call Thatcher," Exitium said.

"We need… at least one of them," Lance said between gasps.

"I'll grab them. You need to get out while you can," Exitium said, kneeling down and pressing something on the side of Lance's head.

"Tell Thatcher to open the portal," He said. Lance nodded, waiting a moment before speaking.

"Thatch, we need a portal, stat," Lance said. Exitium stood back up and walked towards Clay, raising his hand and in turn raising Clay into the air, eye-level.

"Damn…. I was shooting at the wrong one," Lance chuckled, standing up slowly as, in the middle of the circle, a strange black and purple orb appeared from thin air. Lance touched the orb and his body was sucked into it, disappearing before Clay's eyes.

As Exitium approached it, however, he stopped in his tracks when a hand rose from the earth, latching into his leg.

A group of three figures climbed up from the ground, all of them the same color as the dirt they rose from, with blades of grass and roots embedded within their bodies.

Exitium stepped back, looking over the figures before looking up to the top of the ice wall.

Upon the top of it were Sergeants Vander Esch, Alvarez and Johnson, Alvarez with a yellow aura around her hand, seemingly the one who rose the soil-made attackers.

Sergeant Johnson put his hands out, a gold-like aura surrounding them as he spoke.

"Scythe," He said, and from thin air, the handle and blade of a golden scythe formed within his palms. He moved to a fighting stance, hopping down from the ice wall to face Exitium.

Looking over the opposition, Exitium shook his head, looking back at Clay.

"Surface dwellers…" he said. He pumped a tossing motion with his hand, Clay being flung at Johnson before Exitium reached out, grabbing the orb and disappearing into it quickly before the orb dissipated into the air. Clay was caught by the Sergeant, finally blacking out from the hit he had taken before, not long after he was rescued by Titan Squad.

When Clay woke up, Albert was sitting beside his bed, in the infirmary.

"Albert… what happened?" Clay asked.

"I almost had that slimy bastard is what happened… but then that guy with Telekinesis beat us both. Titan squad rescued us, apparently… guess now we know why everyone was bothered that they were there to grade us,"

Albert looked away from Clay as he sat up in bed.

"Now, we're not allowed to leave here until we get word. Engaging with those Magic Users landed us in a lot of trouble, I think. But it would have been worth it if I would've been able to finish him," Albert said, crossing his arms.

Clay looked down at his hands, his brow furrowing.

"Speaking of that Exitium guy... Do you know what happened to him?" Clay asked.

"I think I do,"

Clay and Albert both looked to the opening door as Sergeant Vander Esch came through the door, looking over the brothers, Sergeant Johnson behind him.

Clay and Albert were both in shock, trying to process the information they were given.

"After a couple of practical tests, it seems you two are Magic Users. Your abilities don't show up on the tests we use because it's meta magic, magic that affects other magic. It seems both of you have the ability to suppress magic with your touch,"

Vander Esch was explaining the situation to them, much to their shock and dismay.

"If you grab a Magic User, or even touch them with any part of your arm below the elbow, it seems, their abilities immediately shut down for a while. When you grabbed that cryokinesis user, we saw the fight on our way over and noticed he could have easily used his Ice and froze you, and it looked like he was trying to, but couldn't," The Sergeant said.

"So, what about Exitium?" Clay asked, "when I touched him with my bare knuckles with a punch, he passed out for a while,"

"We're still not familiar with these two Magic Users that attacked you. We have files on most Red Hand members, and they weren't in them. They're either new recruits, or not with them at all," Sergeant Vander Esch said, nodding to Johnson, who put his hand out and spoke.

"Rapier,"

In his hand, a sword formed from thin air, letting the Sergeant grip it.

"Now, go ahead and touch his hand," Vander Esch said, Johnson putting his hand out in front of Clay.

Clay hesitated, before clasping his hand with the Sergeant's, the sword immediately dissipating into the air.

Clay looked back down at his hands a moment, his brow furrowing.

"So… what does this mean? Are we gonna be…?" Clay trailed off, Albert tensing up at the question.

"Well, normal protocol is to take you into custody, ensure your loyalty to Tarren, and hold a trial. I'm not sure when, exactly, this process will start for you two, but I can say one thing. You two fought off two Magic Users without even knowing about your abilities, evidently, in order to protect your fellow trainees. You may have disobeyed orders but you did it for the right reasons, and had you not been Magic Users, most likely you would've given your lives for your allies. I think that you both have a case, and if you make it back into the military, Titan Squad would love to include you," Vander Esch smiled, before there was a knock on the door.

The Sergeant opened the door, Sergeant Oroc standing at it. Him and Vander Esch whispered for a second before Oroc entered, while Vander Esch and Johnson stepped outside, the door closing.

"Are you both okay?" The Instructor asked them. With both of them giving back a "yes, sir" Sergeant Oroc nodded, before taking a breath and beginning his yelling.

"Do you realize how much danger the both of you were in?! How much danger the rest of the class was in?! Had you not fared as well as you did, those two could have had free reign to kill as many people in the class as they wanted! Why did you not at least evacuate the other trainees, or give them the order to evacuate before engaging?!"

Sergeant Oroc yelled at the two trainees for almost an hour before Sergeant Vander Esch finally returned near the end of his intense lecture.

"Sergeant, the, um… the investigation team is here," Vander Esch said.

"Investigation team?" Sergeant Oroc looked to Sergeant Vander Esch, confused for a moment. Vander Esch beckoned him to come outside as two security forces personnel entered the room, along with another man in uniform, a Staff Sergeant. His black hair was slicked back, and his mustache was barely in line with regulation.

"Boys, I just need to ask you a few questions before we head out," The Sergeant said, walking in and sitting across from them.

"I'm Sergeant Menendez, I'll be conducting the investigation around your abilities," He said, eyeing the boys in caution as he sat. His voice had a suspicious tone to it, but he seemed to be trying to be polite while he spoke to them.

Clay nodded, Albert staying still as ever while the Sergeant talked.

"First, I need to know, on record. When did you learn about your abilities?"

Clay was about to speak up when Albert interjected.

"About five minutes ago," Albert said, his arms crossed while he sat in the chair beside Clay.

"So, when the Sergeant told you?" He asked, both of the boys nodding. Clay looked up at Albert a second, Albert's expression hard and unmoving. He had answered fast, Clay thought.

"Alright, did you notice anything strange about your parents when you were younger? Anything that could have led you to believe one or both of them were Magic Users?" Menendez asked next, Clay and Albert both thinking for a while.

"Well, nothing that I know of," Clay said, looking to Albert, who was deep in thought before realization washed over his face.

"The day of the attack on Goldberg… dad fought off two Magic Users to save me, after one of them killed mom," Albert said, "one of them shot fire, had some on his face, but dad grabbed his arm and it all disappeared,"

Menendez was writing things down and nodding as Albert continued,

"The second one turned into some kind of beast, tried to kill him, but dad grabbed him and he turned back to a normal person," Albert said. Clay looked at him for a moment, a concerned look on his face.

"Alright, anything else?" Menendez asked.

"Well… we encountered a wild one at our house not long after that. He tried to fight him off, but it didn't look like his touch did anything to it," Albert said, Menendez leaning forward in his seat.

"You said a wild one? Did you know what two powers it had?" Menendez asked.

"It was some sort of transmutation. He had a blade in place of one of his hands," Albert replied.

"And the other power? Wild Ones already have two," Menendez said.

Albert paused, looking down for a minute.

"No… no, I don't know…" Albert said.

"Well, maybe your father was suppressing the second one so you didn't see. So, what was your father's name?" Menendez asked.

"Richard Barrett," Clay blankly replied, still staring at Albert. Albert looked over at him before looking down, seemingly guilty.

"And your mother's maiden?" Menendez asked.

"Erica Watkins," Clay said again, finally taking his eyes off Albert to look back down.

"Alright… I'll see what the family records show. Maybe we can find out how you two came to be here," Menendez said.

"Sir, with all due respect, Terran has always been our home. We're not outsiders," Clay said, his brow furrowing as he looked at the Sergeant.

"We both signed up and pledged to serve this nation, even if it meant giving our lives. Please don't treat us like invaders," Clay said, his fists balling up and his body tensing until he saw Menendez was the same way, not out of anger, but out of fear. He was afraid of Clay, not because he gave him a reason to be, but simply because he was what he was…

The two security forces both had their hands on their pistols, their feet back in caution.

Clay looked back down, sighing and relaxing, Menendez relaxing a bit as well. The SF stood down as well, looking at each other for just a moment.

"That's all I had. Security Forces, please escort these... *men*... to the MU holding cells," Menendez said, leaving as the SF brought them both to their feet, letting Clay get dressed before they both were taken away.

As they walked out into the infirmary hall, Sergeant Vander Esch was talking to Sergeant Oroc, until their instructor got a look at the two. He froze, watching them go by, a half-afraid, half-angry look on his face. Clay and Albert both looked at him in the eyes as they passed before SF kept them moving forward, around the corner and out of sight of the Sergeants.

It was 2 weeks before the two got to go to trial, one question on their minds that both of them knew would be the deciding factor in whether they would live or die: their loyalty to the nation, and to the Chancellor.

In the span of two weeks, the two of them were interviewed several times, both about their encounter with Lance and Exitium, and about the attack on Goldberg, which Albert knew much more about than Clay.

Before they knew it, the pair of Security Forces who had been giving them their food through a compartment in the wall approached the door, ordering them to step back from the door.

The men entered, grabbing the two and bringing them out into the hall. They ordered them to move, bringing them to one of the base's local Courtrooms, where the whole room was packed with Soldiers, including some of the brothers' classmates and Sergeant Oroc. Also, near the front of the crowd stood Sergeants Alvarez, Vander Esch, and Johnson, of Titan Squad. Vander Esch gave the boys a curt nod, more for good luck than anything else. And in the judge's seat, the same blonde-haired man they had seen on TV right before the attack on Goldberg: the Chancellor of Tarren, Jackson Ambrose.

The courtroom itself was the usual oak room that most trials in Tarren were held in. Rows of seating nearly like pews were railed off from the rest of the room, with 2 tables in front of the rails, one for the defense and one for the prosecution. To the side was a jury pit that currently sat empty, and in front was the Judge's podium, where Chancellor Ambrose now sat.

The Chancellor himself was an older man, roughly in his 60's. Fair skin and hair that had obviously been dyed bleach blonde.

The brothers were led forward to their seats at the table on the left, while their defense and the prosecutor were waiting to begin.

The trial was almost like a battle in and of itself. The defense for the two was handled by a military counsel named Jason Brewer, who Albert whispered to Clay was known to be the same one who advocated for Titan Squad's formation in the first place.

The prosecutor was Frederick Callaghan, a renowned prosecutor whose main argument, in this case, was the attack on Goldberg and Bullpup's report that there was a struggle in town and Albert & Clay's mother had died in it, suggesting that one or both of them, or their father, had participated in the struggle since there was no way a non-Magic-User could put up such a fight against the leader of the Red Hand and his Second in command. Clay and Albert were both called to the stand to testify, both for the defense and prosecution.

"Did you not find it strange that your father, who has the same ability as you, was able to simply grab the Magic User and negate their powers?" Callaghan asked Albert.

"I did wonder why their powers stopped working, but I wasn't sure that it was my dad making it happen," Albert said.

"And you never thought to ask him about what happened later on, after the initial attack?" Callaghan asked.

"I never got the chance between us leaving the store and encountering the wild one at home," Albert replied.

"And when he encountered the wild one, he grabbed him as well?" Callaghan continued.

"Yes, but from what I saw, there was no change. That's why he died. I heard that Wild Ones had two abilities so I believe he was suppressing the second, one that I couldn't see being used," Albert said.

"So, let me ask. How did the wild one kill your father but not you or your brother?" Callaghan edged closer to his point.

"He was holding the Wild one's arm and got stabbed, and he told me to shoot it with his gun he had asked me to get a few minutes before. I shot it a few times and it fell over with its blade still through his chest," Albert said, tears welling up in his eyes but he kept his voice steady. Clay was sitting beside his defense counsel, head in his hands from replaying his own memory of the incident.

"So, let me ask you one final question. Did it ever occur to you that if he hadn't been holding the Wild one when you shot, that it wouldn't have died?" Callaghan finally put the period on his statement.

"I... I don't know," Albert said, looking down as the prosecutor returned to his seat.

"No further questions, Chancellor," Callaghan said.

The trial continued on after Albert sat back down, eventually Brewer called Sergeant Vander Esch to the stand.

"At what time did the military have a suspicion that the defendants were Magic Users?" Brewer asked Sergeant Vander Esch on the stand.

"During the attack on Goldberg by a group of Magic Users, a clean-up squad noticed that there was some sort of struggle at the local supermarket, with one casualty," Vander Esch said.

"And, for the record, who was the casualty?" Brewer noted.

"It was Mrs. Erica Barrett, the mother of the Barrett brothers," Vander Esch clarified,

"But, the squad noted that the flames and claws were consistent with two Magic Users who have a history of violence, Vin Vale and Tristan Lupos, but it wasn't consistent with their usual attacks. There was a major struggle, one that the soldiers never would have expected from someone fighting these two. Whoever it was that fought them either was an extremely skilled combatant, or was some form of Magic User. While that doesn't specifically put them on a suspected Magic-User list, it was the first sign," Vander Esch stated.

"So, what was the second sign?" Brewer asked.

"Well, a dead wild one was found at Mrs. Barrett's home, along with her husband, Mr. Richard Barrett, also deceased. The squad on the scene wrote their report and brought in some research about the family history of both Mrs. and Mr. Barrett. Mr. Barrett's mother had no family record and refused to talk to us over the phone," Vander Esch explained.

The trial lasted for roughly 8 hours before the Chancellor came to a decision.

"Albert and Clay Barrett. One of you signed up for the military before the attack on Goldberg, correct?" Chancellor Ambrose asked.

"Yes, sir, I did," Albert said, both of them standing beside their Counsel.

"Well, after the horrific incidents you both have witnessed, I highly doubt either of you have any ill intent by joining, and it was confirmed only one of your parents was a Magic User, meaning no mental tolls should occur as a result of your powers. With these things in mind, I have reasonable cause to believe you both are loyal to our nation and to myself, so as such, I have no issue with releasing you to the custody of Titan Squad," Chancellor Ambrose said. Albert and Clay were both nearly in tears as they breathed a sigh of relief.

"If I may ask, who was their instructor? Can I see him?" Chancellor Ambrose asked. Sergeant Oroc stepped into the Aisle, going to attention.

"At ease soldier, I simply have a question," The Chancellor said, "did these boys complete their training?" He asked.

"My class, the two Barrett brothers included, has completed all necessary assignments in order to graduate. We still must go through our ceremony, but they are ready to graduate," Sergeant Oroc replied.

"Well then, they may graduate with their class, under the supervision of Titan Squad, and will then be assigned to Titan Squad after graduation," Chancellor Ambrose said, finalizing the decision with a slam of his gavel on the podium in front of him.

◆◆◆◆◆

The graduation ceremony went as usual, with no deviation from the normal ceremony due to Clay or Albert. Both of them stood among their fellow trainees in formation, and as Sergeant Oroc approached them, he gave them their badges certifying them as soldiers, shaking their hands before moving on to the other trainees.

However, after the official ceremony was ready to conclude, that was when the surprise came.

"Ladies and gentlemen, we have learned we have a special guest here with us today who would like to say a few words before we conclude. Please welcome to the stage, Chancellor Jackson Ambrose," Sergeant Oroc said before shaking the man's hand, stepping aside to let Chancellor Ambrose take to the podium.

"Thank you, thank you…" he said to applause,

"I came here not as some sort of precaution, but as a motivator. Every soldier here has a role within our system, and every soldier has something special to offer our armed forces. Be it due to their physical, mental, or other talents, each of them has something they wanted to give to their country in service for something greater than themselves. That is a fact that earns my respect for every single one of them, no matter their race, looks, or other… 'differentiating factors.'" The Chancellor said, obviously referring to the two brothers.

The Chancellor continued his speech, Clay and Albert both pausing as they felt that same sense of Deja Vu, Clay seeing a flash, almost a vision. Fire, explosions… and more death than he had ever seen before.

Clay struggled to keep his back straight and stay on his feet, his whole body shaking as Albert very quickly darted his eyes to look at him.

"That is all I had, thank you so much for listening, and I hope you all can make a difference for Tarren and the world!" Chancellor Jackson said, a huge round of applause and cheers coming his way as he waved, stepping off the podium.

After a few moments, while the trainees were conversing with their families and Chancellor Ambrose shook hands with people, Clay and Albert approached him.

"Sir…?" Clay said, slightly wary.

Chancellor Ambrose looked over and smiled as he saw the two boys, nodding.

"Ah, yes, our newest additions to Titan Squad. Glad to see you are both well," The Chancellor said. Clay put out his hand to shake the Chancellor's just as the Chancellor brought up a handkerchief to clean his own hands off, prompting Clay to let his hand fall to his side.

"I'm greatly looking forward to seeing what the two of you can do. Perhaps with the proper training from Titan Squad, you can use your abilities more efficiently?" The Chancellor said.

Clay and Albert looked to each other for a moment, confused before Albert looked back.

"More efficiently, sir?" He asked.

"Ah, I forgot, neither of you are too educated on the subject of magic. You'll have to talk to Sergeant Vander Esch when you have the chance. He can explain much more about magic than I," Chancellor Ambrose said.

With that, the two of them began forming more and more questions in their minds for when they arrived at Titan Squad's facility, but as Sergeant Johnson stood near the exit of the ceremony, they supposed they wouldn't have to wait long.

Chapter 3

"Yeah, Bullpup and Sergeant Vander Esch have worked together on several missions. Funny enough, these guys are the most open-minded ones we've worked with. Most squads don't take kindly to us just because we're Magic Users,"

The sound of Humvees and Helicopters filled the air as Clay, Albert, and Titan Squad rode towards a military base near the border of Tarren and Brakata. In the distance, gunfire shot constantly, and explosions far away from the base could be heard.

"What are they shooting at...?" Clay asked, looking to Sergeant Vander Esch.

"Well, you don't really hear it on the news that much but efforts to combat the Wild Ones haven't gone too great. The military has held them back so far, but they have become a major problem in Brakata. We're not sure where they're coming from, but Brakata has refused to let us in their country so we can find out," Sergeant Vander Esch said.

The Humvee that held the group entered the base, passed the gates and proceeded into the command complex of the base.

"It's been a while since we've been home..." Johnson said, twirling a bullet between his fingers.

"Yeah, and it's been even longer since we've added to our squad," Alvarez chuckled, looking at the two boys.

"So, what's you guys' story, anyways? I didn't get to hear," she said, leaning forward with her elbows on her knees.

"We were in the attack on Goldberg; both our parents died. Originally, we joined for revenge on Magic Users, but now it's more for the freedom of our nation," Clay said. Albert stayed silent, staring out the window.

"So what, you wanna be some knight in shining armor for Tarren?" Alvarez laughed a bit, and Clay got a bit red in the face.

"Well, I think we could use more guys that come in looking for more than benefits and money," Alvarez said, leaning back in her seat.

"So, what do you mean by freedom?" she asked, bobbing her head up for a second as she stretched her back.

"Well, personally, I just want these random attacks to stop. I don't think anyone should have to live in fear wondering if their town is the next one this 'Red Hand' is targeting," Clay said. Alvarez nodded, looking over at Albert.

"What about you, Mr. Brooding? What made you sign up?" Alvarez asked.

Albert looked up, then thought for a minute, keeping his eyes on the floorboard.

"I signed up before the attack on my hometown… At first, I was just looking for a purpose," Albert answered.

"And now? You've had two encounters with the Red Hand already, have your thoughts changed?" Alvarez asked, her joking tone slowly turning more serious.

"Now… I dunno…" Albert looked back out the window.

"Now, I just want to get rid of the Red Hand. Make sure they can't do to other families what they did to us," Albert said, crossing his arms. Clay could tell he was holding something back, he had something more to say but refused, but Clay wasn't going to force it out of him.

"Very different reasons, but, they both have value in their own way," Alvarez smiled, crossing her arms as Johnson and Vander Esch looked at one another.

"Before we arrive, I should say we usually don't go by last names out here. Call me Julie, you can call Sergeant Johnson by Vincent, and

Sergeant Vander Esch, you can call Adam," Julie said. Both of the brothers nodded in reply.

The Humvee slowed to a stop in the underground parking area underneath the command complex.

The group got out of the Humvee, with all five walking together towards the elevator and taking it up to the third out of five floors.

"This is our headquarters, of sorts," Vincent began, "it's where we come to relax between missions, and where Adam fills out his paperwork for the Capital,"

"Wait, Titan Squad works directly under Chancellor Ambrose?" Clay asked.

"Yep, Adam has a direct line with the Chief of the Magic Suppression Force, which is regulated only by the Chancellor. Oh, and this is also where Julie does... her thing," Johnson waved his hand a bit, gesturing towards Alvarez.

"Hey! Trying to find out more about Magic Users isn't just 'something,' it's a valid pursuit of knowledge," Julie defended, crossing her arms and pouting a bit at Vincent.

"Well, would you rather I call them 'Experiments on Wild Ones?' Because that's roughly what they are," Vincent replied.

"No! Don't call them that, that makes my patients sound like guinea pigs and me sound like some mad scientist!" Julie raised her voice a bit, Vincent looking at her with a sarcastic expression.

"Alright, this is painting a bad picture," Julie looked at Clay and Albert, who had both taken a step back and looked half-scared of the woman.

"Okay okay, calm down. No, I do not experiment on people. It's hard to explain. Maybe I can just show you instead?" Alvarez shrugged, a nervous smile on her face.

Clay slowly took a cautious step forward, nodding a bit.

"Alright... as long as it doesn't hurt anyone, and it helps us learn more about what we are," Clay said. Albert followed behind as the three of them headed down a set of stairs. Johnson and Vander Esch continued on into two different rooms in the hallway they entered from the Elevator.

After 2 flights of stairs and Albert asking why they didn't just go back down the elevator, Alvarez replied "it doesn't stop on this floor; it's sort of a secret spot," The three of them finally arrived at a hallway with glass walls all around, the walls looking into nearly empty rooms, each room holding one person. Most of them had 2 IV's in their arms and were strapped down to their beds with heart monitors and brainwave monitors on them. However, one room held a person simply sitting in the corner, staring at the floor. There were small slots near the floor of every cell and doors on each cell as well.

"What is all this…?" Albert asked, looking into the rooms as Julie walked down the hall, turning on a couple extra lights. On the other side of the room was a computer, a landline phone, and a test tube rack filled with tubes holding different liquids inside. Beside the rack was a microwave…

"This is my medical lab. I've been using this facility to try and, one, find a way to suppress magic abilities, and two, find out what causes a Magic-User to become a wild one," Alvarez stated.

Clay and Albert walked down the hall, observing each room until Clay stopped, looking at the man in the corner. He was shirtless, the shorts on him hugging his waist tightly with the strings that hung down the front of them. His dirty blonde hair was ruffled, his eyes were a yellow-green, and his pupils were extremely large compared to a normal person's.

"What's this guy's story? He's not strapped down like the rest," Clay asked. Albert looked over, and Julie leisurely walking over towards his cell.

"He's… a special case," Alvarez said before perking up a bit.

"Oh crap, I just remembered!" She said, running to a large cabinet and opening it up, the cold air turning to vapor as it flowed into the room. The inside of the cabinet was colder than a freezer.

Alvarez took out a couple TV dinners and walked to the microwave, opening one and preparing it.

"TV dinners?" Clay asked, walking towards her.

"Yeah, for some reason with him, if he can't have Salisbury Steak, he won't eat. So, I have to keep a stock of it. It's cheaper than the nutrient IV's I have the rest of them on, anyways," Alvarez said, taking the TV dinner out and grabbing a plastic fork, walking it over to the room and opening it. The man inside looked up, slowly standing as Alvarez handed him the tray. He looked at it a moment, staring into the meat of the Salisbury steak as Alvarez exited the room, shutting the door again.

"He won't eat with people looking at him, so both of you, come here," Alvarez said. At her request, Clay and Albert followed her to her computer, where she was looking over some reports from when she was gone.

"So, I'll make this short, so I won't bore you, but if you want to know more, all you need to do is ask. Basically, I've deduced that within every Magic User is an amount of what I call 'mana' in their blood, mana being a concentrated, liquid form of pure magic,"

Clay and Albert both listened intently, watching her screen as she pulled up a log of brainwave activity from her "Patients,"

"That mana is within the blood as soon as it's injected into a person's blood stream, but it diffuses into their blood, so you can't just take some person's blood and give it to someone else to give them the same magic abilities," Alvarez explained, then pointing to the charts of the patients' brainwaves individually.

"But when two Magic Users reproduce, it is a 50/50 shot on whether the child grows up normally and simply inherits both abilities or the amount of mana along with the knowledge they have two powers overwhelms the mind and causes the Double User, as I've begun to call them, to be driven insane. They become obsessed with one aspect of their lives that they lose, and decide they'll do anything to get to that aspect. Maybe a brother looking for his other sibling, or a lazy person simply wanting to relax and not work for anything. They begin searching for something, and once they find that thing, they either come down from their psychotic state, and return to sanity, or they seem to simply… die. No cause, no reason, they simply fall asleep and their heart stops," Alvarez said. Clay and Albert looked at one another for just a moment, Albert thinking about the Wild One, or the Double User, he supposed, that he had killed after his father engaged it.

"Our dad, he was killed by one…" Albert said. Alvarez looked back at him with interest.

"I heard at the trial, something like that… Do you remember much about what happened?" Julie asked. Clay was staring at Albert again, only thinking about the lie that Albert had told him regarding their mother.

"There was only one word I heard it say, 'Jason…' I assume it was the name of a loved one before it lost its mind," Albert said.

"Well… there's not much of a chance we could find whoever 'Jason' is, but at least it's something," Alvarez shrugged.

"It's something to show you that a lot of these Double Users aren't monsters, and neither are the standard Magic Users, for that matter. There used to be a lot of good ones along with the bad ones you are used to…" Alvarez said, looking back to the computer.

"Well, we didn't learn much about the Great Wars back in school or during our basic training. Do you know much about it?" Clay asked.

As they stared, Alvarez slowly lowered her head before snapping her face towards them. Her expression lit up like a Christmas tree.

"Clay. I thought you'd never ask! Oh, where do I start? From the first Great War? How Clemence became a superpower? The infamous battle of D-day?!" Alvarez exclaimed before the landline phone on her desk began to ring. Alvarez looked over and hit the button to answer the speaker.

"Julie," Johnson spoke, "Need you and the rookies to the main deck immediately. We have some trouble,"

The two and Alvarez went back up the stairs and entered the hallway, then went down a secondary hall and into a large, spacious room with 4 desks in it and windows running all along one side in a half-circle, stopping at the final wall behind the three.

"What's the issue?" Alvarez asked, Johnson and Vander Esch already in the room looking over a screen.

"Brakata pushing more and more Wild Ones our way," Vander Esch said, "We're still not sure where they're coming from, but they're routing them all towards the border. Unless they break off from the small group that's there, none of them are actually being shot at,"

Alvarez looked over the screen, cursing under her breath.

"That's like 30 of them. If just one has a destructive enough power, we could be in deep trouble," Alvarez said, crossing her arms.

"The Suppression force already has a couple squads on the way, but they want us in for casualty control," Johnson looked over at her, speaking while he leaned forward on the desk.

"Well, let's go, then!" Alvarez said, jogging to the door, followed by Johnson before both of them looked back. Vander Esch was standing beside the two brothers with his arms crossed, shooting an annoyed expression at the two of them.

"We need to gear these two up beforehand. If any of them has a ranged attack in their arsenal, these two are defenseless, and if they get mobbed, they're done for," Vander Esch said. Johnson and Alvarez both agreed before they stopped to get the brothers dressed in standard equipment. Once they were ready, Titan Squad began heading out to the site.

The land around the base was green plains all the way to the Border with Brakata, where a forest was cut off right at the border. Trees almost lined Brakata's side of the trench that separated the two countries. Out in the distance, past the forests and plains, trails of steam belched out from the horizon from the field of Geysers that stretched from Brakata all the way across Tarren's mainland.

Johnson and Alvarez looked over the group of Wild Ones walking towards the base. the group was spread out over a wide area, each of them looking around in confusion. They were all dressed in torn and worn-out clothing, most of it extremely old-fashioned. All of the women were in dresses, and the men wore vests and pants that had a waistband above their belly buttons. All of the Double Users were of young adult age. Most likely, none of them were over the age of 25.

"I can see about 16 of them walking away from the bridges that span the trench," Alvarez said.

Johnson looked over a couple of the ones who turned back, walking towards the trench and towards Brakata. One stepped onto the bridge, and the sounds of bullets popping and gunshots rang out, about 10 shots firing into the Double User before it hit the wood floor of the bridge, Brakata soldiers dragging it into their land a second later and disappearing with it behind the trees.

"They're murdering the ones that turn back…" Alvarez said, shaking her head. Albert looked to her before looking down at the defenses that stood not far from the base, and the soldiers manning them.

"Isn't that what we're doing as well?" Albert asked. Clay watched the border despite not being able to see too much besides the figures walking from the border.

"Our job isn't extermination," Sergeant Vander Esch said, his arms crossed as he looked over the border, "it's to subdue them, maybe try to find what it is their minds are fixated on. Maybe we can find a way to bring them down from their obsession and bring them back to Earth, mentally,"

"Or," Sergeant Alvarez spoke up, "if we can't get them what they're looking for, we hold them in my lab so I can hopefully find a way to bring them down another way. That's the last resort before…" she trailed off, looking down.

"Before they're sent to the Capital," Johnson said.

"What do they do to them at the Capital?" Clay asked, looking over at the Sergeant.

"None of us know, exactly. But the Chancellor visits the MSF facility in the Capital fairly often, and none of the Double Users that enter the Capital facility ever leave," Alvarez said, looking down. Sergeant Vander Esch looked at her for a moment, walking over and resting a hand on her shoulder as he observed the group of Double Users headed their way.

"That's why it's our job to subdue them and do our best to bring their minds back to reality," Vander Esch said, "But it's a dangerous job, a lot of the time. They don't take kindly to people getting in their way, and the few that fixate on things like chaos and destruction… there's not much we can do against them,"

Johnson cracked his neck, rolling his shoulders for a second as he got ready.

"Case in point, what's about to happen," Johnson said, looking back at Vander Esch.

"Yep, let's not waste any more time. Vincent, Julie. Keep an eye on Clay and Albert while you fight. Make sure they don't get into trouble," Vander Esch said.

"I can't get over that first name business," Albert muttered.

"We're much more than just field comrades, boys," Alvarez said, chuckling, "we've been friends for years. It may not be the usual, but it's how we roll,"

Johnson nodded, putting his hand out and speaking.

"Baton,"

A yellow shine came from his hand and soon, a steel baton formed in his grip.

"Do we know where these Double Users are all coming from? I thought both Brakata and Tarren had ordered Magic Users to be exterminated," Clay asked.

"They did. We don't know where they're coming from, just like here in Tarren. They all just seem to appear, mostly near the borders but once in a while on the mainland too," Johnson said as Vander Esch outstretched his hands, a red aura surrounding them.

Vander Esch made a circle with one hand, opening a red, circular portal that led to the field just behind the moving Magic Users.

"Julie, stick with Clay. Vincent, with Albert. With these two, our jobs might be a lot easier. Clay, Albert, focus on grabbing your targets and shutting down their most powerful ability. Julie and Vincent, keep on offense and subdue them and bring them to me. I'll transport them to our empty cells back at the base," Adam said, as the group was walking through the portal.

"Wait, I thought the cells in Al… in Julie's cells were full?" Clay said as they looked over the backs of the Double Users in front of them.

"We have dozens underground. Those are just my active cases," Julie said, shrugging, "One I even think I've helped pretty well. He just can't talk, unfortunately," She said, her voice clearly disappointed.

"If I could just get one to have a conversation with me, I could find out more about where they're coming from," She said, kneeling down and touching the dirt beneath her and mumbling something to herself.

In front of the Double Users, a line of humanoid figures rose from the ground, all of them made from grass and dirt.

Most of the Double Users were confused, looking over the figures and studying them, walking around them to observe, while three of them looked at the dirt figures and immediately attacked.

The first swung, driving its fist through the earthen person before grabbing its head and ripping it off, leaving the dirt to fall back to the ground, the body dissolving.

The second had a tail, his skin a sickly green color as he turned and struck the dirt man with the extra appendage, ripping him in half with the tail.

The third looked over the figure before it…

"Nathan…" the wild one said, one of his arms in the shape of a blade, the material of his finger nails making up the blade's edge as he stabbed the earth figure.

Clay and Albert stared at the last wild one as Vander Esch spoke again.

"Those three take priority. Vincent," Adam said, looking to Vincent as he closed the portal.

Sergeant Johnson nodded in response and walked forward, gesturing for Albert to follow him.

Albert was hesitant, but moved forward with Vincent, geared up the same as Clay, with body armor and a pepper ball rifle, with his dad's old 1911 strapped to his hip, fully loaded. Clay had the same gear, only with a G-17 on his hip instead.

"I'll keep this first one's attention, just focus on grabbing him and holding on while I subdue him," Vincent said to Albert, his baton still in his hand as he approached the first wild one.

"When you grab him, try to target one of his powers and shut it down!" Vincent said, the Wild one turning to them and swinging at Vincent.

He moved to the side, tossing his baton to his other hand and slamming it against the back of the Wild One's head. Albert jumped forward, dropping his rifle and grabbing the back of the wild one's neck.

Through his arm, he felt two pulses of electricity, though neither of them hurt. He could feel two completely different kinds of feelings in his arm. One of them flowed through his fingers. It was solid, like he was touching a rock. The other feeling shot through his thumb; it felt like it was petrifying, like his whole arm was turning to the branch of a tree.

Albert focused on the rock-like feeling, pushing against it until the feeling faded. The wild one struggled against him as he forced it to the ground on its stomach, handcuffing the wild one's hands behind its back.

"Julie! The dampener!" Vincent yelled. Julie took out a small, circular device from one of her pockets. It had a red light in the middle, and the back had 3 thin needles sticking out.

"We have five. Make them count!" She yelled, tossing it to Vincent before he stabbed it into the back of the wild one.

"What is that?" Albert said, standing and letting go of the wild one cautiously, Vincent doing the same.

"It's a magic dampener," Julie replied, her hands on the ground as she made more dirt figures for the Double Users to study, or destroy.

"They were made during the second Great War to take prisoners from battles. They were the only way the world could keep Magic Users from killing their would-be captors, but they don't work on chronic powers, and only drain the power for a short time, making it less potent," Vincent explained, and Albert nodded. Clay zoned out just for a second to think over the device as Albert and Vincent looked to the next Wild One that was attacking dirt men.

"Don't grab this one's tail, if you end up shutting its mutations down, it may cause you to lose contact," Vincent said to Albert as they approached. The Wild One looked at them both before a pair of dirt people grabbed it from behind, one grabbing its tail, the other pulling its arms around the Wild One's arms in a full nelson.

"Now!" Vincent yelled. Julie tossed him another dampener as Albert ran for him. Clay and Julie moved to the third Double User. Julie sprang up 4 more dirt figures to try and hold him down while they moved in with the dampener.

"Where… is Nathan…?" The Double User asked, skewering the head of another dirt man onto his blade hand before it sunk back into the earth.

Julie stopped and kneeled to the ground, touching the earth and raising 3 more men from the ground, all of them immediately running at the Double User with the blade for a hand. Clay flanked to the side and approached the Double User, observing it as he got closer behind it. The Double User watched the three earthen beings approach him, readying himself. As they got close enough, the Double User jumped to the side, twisting his body to the left, the blade on his left hand spinning through the air before he sliced the first dirt man from shoulder to hip. The Double User then ran across to the second, wrapping his arm around its neck and bringing his blade up to the dirt man's head.

"Where is my brother?!" He said, threatening the dirt figure while staring at the third, who had backed off a bit.

Clay jumped on the back of the Double User, putting his arm around its throat in the same manner it had the dirt man, his other arm swinging around so he could lock his hold in by grabbing his upper arm while his left arm grabbed the back of the Double User's blade hand.

On contact, two feelings shot through his hand and up his arm. The first, a metallic, sharp feeling, like a knife carved up his arm, but without the pain. The second...

Clay's eyes widened, realizing what the second power was before the Double User threw its head back and slammed it into Clay's nose. Clay fell off the Double User, holding his nose before looking up at the foe.

It swung its blade down, cutting off the legs of the dirt man and throwing him to the ground before jumping forward at the second, slicing its head off. The Double User turned back to the first dirt man, who was struggling to get back up without his legs. He jumped up, raising the blade up before lunging, stabbing it into the dirt man and reducing it to a pile of soil on the ground.

Just as the Double User was approaching Clay, Albert yelled out at him.

"Jason!"

The Double User turned to Albert, confirming his suspicions.

"Your brother, Nathan... he's been looking for you, you know!" Albert yelled. Jason began walking towards Albert and Vincent, who had traded his baton out for a shortsword.

"I was wondering who Jason was whenever I met him... guess now we know," Albert said, slowly lowering his hand to his hip, and to his 1911.

Clay slowly stood, walking around to the side, out of the way as he watched Jason's movements.

"Do you know where he is?" Jason asked.

"Yeah… I do…" Albert said, "Nathan killed my dad, you know? He killed him looking for you," Albert called out to Jason.

"I don't control him… but in my search for him, I'm willing to do the same," Nathan said, planting his back foot about 15 feet from Albert and Vincent.

"Now where is my brother?!" Jason yelled.

Albert's eyes darted to Clay for just a moment, his hand slowly clasping around his 1911.

Julie pulled the two detained Double Users through one of Vander Esch's portals as Albert gave his reply.

"After he killed my dad, I killed him…" Albert admitted. Jason looked down, his eyes moving from his hand to his blade arm and back again for just a moment.

"Did he… did he use his second ability?" Jason asked with tears in his eyes. He raised his head to face Albert again, his expression turning from sad to angry.

"No, he didn't… because you're still here," Jason said, gritting his teeth. Clay's eyes widened as he yelled to Albert and Vincent.

"Don't let him use his second! He turns himself into a bomb!" Clay yelled, running at Jason.

Jason darted forward at Albert. Vincent jumped in the way as Jason raised his blade, while Albert brought his gun out but didn't aim as Vincent was in the way. Jason and Vincent clashed, the edges of their blades both chipping slightly and locking into one another. Jason and Vincent both pushed, grabbing the backs of their blades for more leverage. Vincent began to overpower the wild one before he pushed both of their blades to the side.

Vincent lost his sword and stumbled to the side, Jason twisting his body and bringing up his sword to deliver a blow to Vincent's back.

Before he could finish it, however, Clay grabbed him again, his blade retreating and his arm becoming normal.

Jason looked at his arm as it slammed down on Vincent's back, knocking him to the ground. Jason looked back to Clay, who had a hold of his neck again, now ignoring the shock he had felt at first and focusing on negating his blade.

Jason looked at Albert again, over his shoulder.

Jason balled his fists, a glow beginning to emit from his stomach. Clay saw the glow and his eyes widened, turning his focus to it, but letting his blade return again.

Jason raised his blade up and shoved the edge down into Clay's foot, causing him to yell in pain and let his grip go. Jason lunged forward, away from Clay before turning and bringing his blade in, preparing to stab him.

Albert saw Jason's actions and remembered what Nathan had done to his father…

Before he could finish Clay, Albert fired a round into the shoulder of the wild one. Jason fell to a knee from the shot, the glow returning, and quickly. Clay jumped forward to try and grab him again while Julie helped Vincent up, Albert moving forward to join them, keeping his gun trained on Jason.

Just before Clay could grab the wild one, a portal opened up in front of him. Clay sprinted through it before he realized he had been transported back onto the roof of the HQ. Vander Esch was standing nearby, closing it behind him.

Another opened as Albert fired again, the bullet drilling into Jason's leg before Albert was pulled back through the portal by Vincent and Julie.

"Nathan… I'll see you soon…" Jason said, before erupting in a ball of flame, the portal closing just before the fire reached it.

Clay looked back as a huge ball of fire expanded from the point Jason once stood, engulfing most of the Double Users in the area, minus the two that Julie and Vincent had already pulled to the HQ.

"Oh, my God…" Julie said, covering her mouth as she looked over the explosion. A colossal plume of smoke rose into the air, away from the blast. Through even more smoke, they saw The grass was charred to nothing, and not a trace of any of the Double Users they had seen before. Several trees on Brakata's side of the border had been uprooted, charred and flung away from the trench, landing somewhere else in the woods.

Clay fell to a knee, leaning on the ledge and keeping pressure off his stabbed foot while he observed the damage. The shockwave from the explosion hit the building and almost knocked most of Titan squad to the ground, windows inside smashing all over the place.

"Lord…" Albert said, standing and seeing what the explosion had done, "this is what dad was saving us from… he didn't just save us, he also saved the city and a lot of people around it," Albert said.

"This is why we meet them here… some of their powers are so destructive, Brakata decided it's easier to let us deal with them rather than do anything themselves," Sergeant Vander Esch said, still standing with his arms crossed, "make no doubt about it… until we find a way to help them, Wild Ones are our enemy. We may not fight to kill, but they do, and we can't hold back if it comes down to this again,"

Clay and Julie both looked down, pondering the Sergeant's words while Albert and Vincent both nodded in agreement, Albert's brow furrowing while he watched over the destruction.

The two Wild Ones that Titan squad had captured were put into a set of holding cells underground, awaiting treatment from Julie.

Albert had returned to his quarters, cleaning his 1911 after telling Clay, "The damn thing needs a new trigger bar…"

Clay joined Julie in the lab, looking back over her data about her current patients.

"So, about everything we were talking about earlier…" Clay said, rubbing his neck.

"Oh yeah, what did you want to know about?" Julie asked, looking back at Clay.

"Well, first, what else have you learned about magic abilities? Albert and I don't really know much about our powers, or any others, for that matter,"

Julie nodded, looking back to her computer and pulling up a couple of word documents she had obviously been writing for a while.

"Well, to know about Magic Users and their powers, the most important thing for me was to find out where they came from. Clemence first discovered magic in the form of something called 'Pennington's Serum,' some sort of liquid energy. We don't know where they found it, but Clemence soon found out that if you inject it into your bloodstream, the stuff fuses with your blood and somehow gives you magical properties. We don't know exactly what the power that you receive is based off of, but we know it's hereditary, so if you have a power, your kid will have the same one," Julie explained.

"So, what did they do with it?" Clay asked.

"They injected their military with it. A hundred thousand people were given special abilities after receiving this injection, and they used these Magic Users, along with their incredible warfare strategy, to conquer a quarter of the world, the territory of Tarren and Brakata included," Julie replied.

"Yeah, I remember talking about how Clemence couldn't be beaten for 20 years because of their ranks being Magic Users, but I wasn't sure of their origin," Clay said.

"Then do you remember much about how the second Great War ended?" Julie asked, looking back at him.

"I remember a bunch of the top-ranking military and government leaders disappeared when Clemence was invaded," Clay said, looking down to Julie as he stood above her seat, then looked back to the computer.

"That's right, but it wasn't just leaders. There was some sort of strange disappearance in Clemence, as if thousands of Clemence citizens suddenly fell off the face of the Earth. It's believed that one of the King's hands used their power to kill all these people, but their power caused them to somehow disintegrate, leaving no trace of them behind," Julie explained.

"So when Clemence was invaded, there was no resistance…" Clay put it together, nodding.

"Exactly. That's why the genocide of Magic Users for the Western Alliance was so easy. Because there was no organization for them, most of them simply fought for survival, in self-defense," Julie said.

"Yet they were all put down, simply because the world saw them as a threat…" Clay surmised, looking down.

Julie only nodded in reply.

"Well, we at least know there are a few good Magic Users in the world. Maybe there are more, somewhere out there? Can't we do something to try and turn people's opinions about them?" Clay asked, turning to the center of the lab, just in front of the cells and beginning to pace, deep in thought.

"I wish it were that simple," Julie said, turning in her chair and crossing her arms, "but Chancellor Ambrose hasn't helped the situation. Aside from us, he's made it clear that he believes all Magic Users are a threat to us, and they should either be killed or shipped to the Capital so they can do God-knows-what to them," She said, huffing.

"Well, can't we advocate for them somehow? Tell him that Magic Users aren't as bad as we first thought?" Clay asked, still pacing and no longer facing Julie as he spoke.

"We've tried plenty of times, trust me. The Chancellor is beyond reason in this," Julie stated.

"Well, what about the public? We could gain a reputation with people and tell them we're Magic Users, surely we could make the case that we're not all that bad," Clay suggested.

"One of the terms of Titan squad is we don't let the public, or worse, the media or news, in on the fact we ARE Magic Users. If we tell the press, our squad will be shut down, and then…" Julie looked down, bringing her index finger up in a thoughtful pose and covering her mouth with the middle of it.

"Actually, since you're here, I had an idea I wanted to try. The one conscious over there," she gestured to the man in the corner, "he was the one that I have learned the most from so far. He was the one who led me to figure out what Anchors are and what his anchor was. Anchors are the things that a Double User fixates on that bring them down from their psychotic states," Julie explained to Clay, who was listening intently.

The Double User in the glass room turned his head to face the two at the desk, slowly walking over to that side of his room, as close as he could get to them.

"I believe that his anchor is knowledge. I don't know how he ever got an education, being a Double User, but I do know that whenever I begin talking about things like this, about him, about Double Users," she said, turning back to look at him, Clay turning back as well.

"He's always listening in," She said smugly.

The man's eyebrows jumped up before he quickly turned away from them, pressing his bare back up against the glass.

"Well, unless he's eating, of course," Julie chuckled as she walked towards his door.

"Hey, grab that chair from the desk and bring it over," she said to Clay before opening his door. Clay rolled the desk chair into the containment room, where Julie gestured for the man to sit.

"Alright, buddy. I have something I want to try. Won't be painful, I promise!" she said, putting one hand on her heart and the other up with three fingers up. "Scout's honor," she added, chuckling a bit.

The Double User shook his head leisurely before having a seat on the chair. Julie kneeled in front of him and had Clay kneel beside her, on his right while she was on his left.

"I heard you were able to feel from touching 'Jason' what his powers were," she said to Clay. He nodded, and she smiled, taking the Double User's hand and presenting it to him.

"Tell me what his abilities are, and see if we can bring him to a point he can speak with us," she said.

Clay nodded, clasping onto the man's hand and feeling what he could.

Two feelings shot through his arm… the first, scales, and a sickly green liquid… qualities of a snake. The second… felt like his blood was being purified, some sort of toxin purification. But… something was strange.

"He has a connection with snakes, and some sort of toxin negation… but the abilities are colliding. It's… painful," Clay said, looking into the man's eyes, "He's in pain, all the time… I think he has venom just like a snake, but his other power is constantly negating it," Clay continued. Julie nodded, her eyes never leaving the man's face. The Double User's head dropped. Julie finally turned back to Clay.

"Can you get rid of his snake characteristics? Maybe then he can speak, and it may get rid of his venom glands, give him some relief," Julie said. Clay focused on the scaly, toxic feeling, pushing it away, out of him.

The Double User winced, groaning. His eyes changed, turning a deep blue, and as he gritted his teeth, Julie noticed two of them were reduced in size.

"Ow…" the man said, holding his jaw. Julie gasped, putting her hand over her mouth.

"My God… that's some ability you have, Clay," the man chuckled. Clay smiled brightly in response.

"Thank you, Mr…?" He trailed off, looking down a second.

"Call me Carter," he said. Julie was still in shock as she heard him speak.

"It worked…" Julie finally said as Carter turned to her.

"Yes, it seems so… I know there's probably a lot you want to ask, so please, just one question at a time. It's been years since I've actually spoken, so I'd like to… take my time," Carter said, blinking a few times. "My God, this is what you two see all the time? I hardly see more than two colors at a time…" Carter said, taking a breath and turning his body towards Julie, his hand still held in Clay's.

"So, what do you want to talk about first?" he asked. Julie thought for a moment, while Clay was simply taking in what he could from their talk as Julie finally asked her first question.

"This one is more personal. But if you are always in pain from your toxin negation burning away your venom, why do you always refuse the sedatives?" she asked. Carter nodded, listening closely before he replied.

"Well, I feel like this pain is part of my existence. I know it's gone right now, which is a giant relief to me, but when I'm not in contact with him, I'll go right back to that pain. It's not something I feel I should run away from, simply because it's a part of me," he explained. Julie gave him a somewhat annoyed look.

"We have power dampeners. They won't get rid of your snake characteristics, but they'll somewhat dampen your toxin negation so you don't have to be in as much pain," she said. Carter stared at her for a moment before they both suddenly laughed at the situation.

"Well, I'd definitely like to try one of them," Carter said, still chuckling. Julie nodded before asking her second question.

"So, why the Salisbury steaks, by the way?" She asked.

Carter gave a thought to this one before he spoke.

"Well, I need meat in my diet, more than anything. Or eggs, but I prefer meat. And Salisbury steaks seemed to be the cheapest form of meat around here. See, my 'Anchor,' as you called it, isn't knowledge; that's not why I always listen when I hear you speak about us. See, before I was here, I remember I always wanted someone to see me, to notice or acknowledge my presence. Since I've been here, you've been feeding me, studying me, wanting to help me… I think someone paying attention to me is what steadied my mind,"

Julie blushed a bit as Carter kept talking.

"But, I supposed you worked hard enough; something easy for you to cook so you can spend more time doing what you need to is better than you laboring to cook for me," Carter looked down, chuckling a bit before Julie stood out of nowhere.

"Well, If that's the only reason, then tomorrow evening I'm cooking you a big steak!" Julie exclaimed, her expression beaming with joy.

Carter looked up, chuckling. "Well, if you insist, just don't overdo yourself," Carter said. Julie paused, thinking, before she sighed, kneeling again.

"I suppose now, we should get to some business talk," she said, taking a more serious tone now.

"Do you know where you came from?"

Clay was up half the night on his phone, looking up things about snakes and their anatomy. Pit organs, their vision, and their venom glands, among other things.

From time to time, Clay would look across from him at Albert, in his bed, his 1911 sitting on his nightstand, loaded magazine beside it, while the gun itself was empty. Clay sighed as he thought about what had happened that day, between the conversation with Carter, to the encounter with Jason and the explosion... a lot had happened in one day, more than he would like, in a way. But with all the bad, a lot of good came from it, too.

Clay checked the time... 2343 hrs, almost midnight. He put his phone aside, rolled onto his back and stared at the ceiling before his vision got blurry. Was he that tired? No... something was wrong. Just like he and Albert had felt before Exitium and Lance appeared, it almost felt like... things around him were changing, deviating from... something.

Clay sat up, turning to Albert, who was still asleep... but his gun and the magazine were missing.

Clay slipped out of bed, putting his boots on and quickly lacing them before he walked out into the hallway just in time to hear a single gunshot come from downstairs.

Clay quickly ran downstairs to Julie's lab, crouching and quietly moving down as he heard two voices: Lance and Exitium.

"Well, we cleaned up that mess. Wonder why we were sent to kill this sorry wild one?" Lance said.

"Apparently had we not, it would have been disastrous. Do not question *his* logic," Exitium replied.

"Yeah, yeah, I know, preventative measures, this and timeline that. We going after the Red Hand now? I'd like to kill something that'll actually fight back," Lance replied.

Their footsteps led down the hall, away from the staircase.

"That's our next stop. There's a geyser not far away we can stop by," Exitium said before Clay jumped down, standing tall at the end of the hallway.

As his boots landed, both of them quieted down and looked back at him, Lance holding Albert's 1911.

Clay said nothing, only staring the two down before Lance chuckled.

"Are you stupid or something? I heard the Lewis family was reckless, but never heard of them being stupid," Lance mocked. Exitium stared Clay down, not saying a word.

"*Lewis family?*" Clay thought, tilting his head to the side just slightly, before Lance spoke again.

"Grab him. We can bring him back too. Two birds with one portal," Lance said. Exitium reached his hand out, Clay felt a grip on his torso that began pulling him towards them. The grip was lifting him into the air, just enough for his feet not to reach the ground.

"Hey Scotty, beam me up," Lance said with a finger in his ear, Exitium turning his head to him.

"Who is Scotty?" he asked.

"Ah, it's just a reference from some TV show they have up here. This guy probably knows what I mean," Lance said, gesturing to Clay, who was still struggling to get out of Exitium's grip.

"You know that their materials are banned back home," Exitium said flatly.

"What can I say? I'm a sucker for sci-fi," Lance said, swirling his wrist around with the gun in it, " There's DVD players and TV's all over the black market back home. I should show you some of my stash sometime. You know what they say, Hokey religions and ancient weapons are no match for a-"

"Who is they?" Exitium interrupted.

"Ugh, nevermind," Lance said, annoyed.

An orb appeared before them, similar to the one that they had used to escape from Titan Squad in the compound near Rotun.

Clay desperately struggled against Exitium's hold, being brought towards the orb before Exitium himself looked back, raising an arm as a throwing knife sunk into his armor. Black and green smoke trailed from the wound as Lance and Clay both looked back to see Vincent and Julie at the end of the hallway.

"You're not taking him anywhere!" Julie yelled, pulling out a pistol as Johnson conjured another throwing knife and threw it at Exitium.

The armored telekinesis user ducked and let the blade sink into the metal floor behind him. Lance got behind a corner of the containment rooms.

"Hey, we got what we came for. Forget the Descendant. Let's go!" Lance yelled to Exitium, who was pulling sheets of metal in the wall to use as cover for himself and Lance.

"Fine… but now we know where he is," Exitium said. Lance looked to the 1911 in his hand, tossing it aside before he and Exitium touched the orb and disappeared, dropping the metal and Clay a second after.

Clay sputtered for a moment as Exitium nearly squeezed the breath from him as he left. The orb disappeared as he struggled to get back to his feet. Julie ran to him, checking him and making sure he was alright.

"Were those the same guys who attacked you and Albert at Rotun?" she asked. Clay nodded, leaning up against one of the containment rooms while he got his bearings.

"Were they after you again?" Julie asked. Clay shook his head before Vincent chimed in.

"I think they completed their objective..." he said.

Julie walked back to see what he was talking about, and saw Carter's containment room door open and Carter lying dead on the ground, a single bullet wound in his chest. A pool of blood surrounded him, trailing from the wound, and a bit more from his mouth as his eyes sat, glazed over, staring at the ceiling.

Julie stood frozen, staring at Carter's body. His dampener was deactivated, no longer functioning on the corpse.

"Carter..." Julie said, stepping into the room to see if he was truly gone.

Julie dropped to her knees, tears in her eyes as she held Carter's body.

"The Red Hand doesn't want us having any more information on Magic Users... or more importantly, where they're coming from..." Vincent said.

"That wasn't the Red Hand..." Clay corrected, slowly bringing himself to stand on his own strength. Vincent looked over, raising an eyebrow as Clay finally got up.

"Then who was it?" Vincent asked. Sergeant Vander Esch walked downstairs, with Albert right behind him as they listened in.

"These guys... they said after they left here that they were going to look for the Red Hand. They're not working for them," Clay said.

"A new group of Magic Users... this presents all-new problems..." Sergeant Vander Esch said.

"Well, whoever they are, they just killed our best chance at figuring out where the Red Hand, and maybe where they, too, are coming from," Vincent said.

Clay walked into the containment room with Julie, kneeling beside her and putting a hand on her shoulder as she cried.

Sergeant Johnson and Albert both looked at them before heading back upstairs, Albert retrieving his 1911 as he asked Vincent what had happened. Vincent began explaining what he saw as they fell out of earshot upstairs.

Vander Esch stood outside as Clay comforted Julie, both of them eventually exiting the containment room.

"I'm sorry this happened…" Sergeant Vander Esch said.

"But if what Mr. Carter told us is true, we need to act quickly," He followed up with.

"Of course…" Julie said, looking back at his body for a moment.

"We'll get another squad and move out to explore this geyser as soon as possible," Adam said.

✦✦✦✦✦

Chapter 4

"The Red Hand launched an attack on the Heart of Tarren, our Capital, and as a result, 26 brave soldiers from the Magic Suppression Force gave their lives. The Red Hand, along with some new recruits to their ranks, attacked a convoy of trucks and attempted to bring wholesale destruction to the city around them. Although there were no civilian casualties, this latest attack is the last that I will allow Tarren to witness...."

Carter sat in the chair with Clay clasping his hand, thinking as he spoke to Julie.

"I don't remember much about my life before I came here. During my childhood, I went to school with a bunch of other Magic Users. Some could throw fire, and others had characteristics of animals... a few could even mess with the senses of others, their sight, their hearing, or smell. But each had a different power, unless they were blood-related, of course," Carter said. Julie hung on every word after having gotten her phone and began recording.

"I remember... I could look outside the windows. But no matter what time it was, it was always dark outside. The city I grew up in had oil lamps all over town, but you never saw a star in the sky, never felt the sunlight on your skin... I don't know why," Carter said.

"I remember... The adults watched kids like us, said we were dangerous, the Double Users... and we were banished once we were old enough. After that... I don't remember much. It was dark, for a long time, I never saw any light... I relied on my senses to find food, but it wasn't much more than scraps from... somewhere...," Carter struggled to remember.

"I do remember the first time I saw sunlight, felt it on my skin… it was about a year ago. I think I was about 18 or so, though I lost track of time in the dark. I remember… Geysers. They were near me when I woke up. I'm not sure how I got there, but I was in a field, with geysers nearby. Before that, everything was hazy… there was some guy there before I fell asleep. He said it was time to 'send them out'… I don't know what he meant, but I fell asleep and woke up in the geyser field, with a bunch of other Double Users. We all wandered around, survived for a year or so before a bunch of soldiers chased us into the forest, and eventually to the field that I was picked up by you guys," Carter said.

"Geysers…" Julie said, thinking, "Do you think they were the ones on the other side of Brakata? I know out East, a string of geysers runs along the East side of Brakata into Tarren. I'm not sure how far into Brakata it goes, but I know it's a huge field of them,"

Clay nodded, thinking as well.

"Maybe we can move to the ones in our territory and See if there's anything there?" Clay said, Julie nodding in agreement.

"Thank you, Carter. If there's anything you need, you just have to ask," Julie said, gently putting her hands around his free one.

"Well, your company and seeing your work is enough for me, now. Though that steak does sound pretty nice," He chuckled, and Julie laughed a bit with him before standing.

"I'll get you that dampener to see if it'll ease your pain, and we can talk more in the morning. Until then, I'll give you a pen and some paper to write down anything else you think of between now and then," She smiled at him before she and Clay left, his mouth and eyes returning to the snake-like form they were before.

Everyone got up the next morning, with motivation, determination and some anger in their hearts, a couple of them with more of the latter than others. Sergeant Vander Esch contacted the MSF, requesting their deployment across the country to the Geysers. Not long after, Titan Squad was called to a meeting in the control center.

"The Chancellor has asked to personally discuss this venture with us," Sergeant Vander Esch said, joining a call that connected and immediately began to ring an unknown number through a projector on Vander Esch's desk connected to his laptop. The other desks were arranged so the laptop camera could see everyone in the room as they sat together.

Soon enough, Chancellor Ambrose's face was projected on the screen as he sat at his desk.

"Ah, there we are! Hello, Sergeant Vander Esch, hello Titan Squad," The Chancellor said, a smile on his face as he greeted everyone, who gave their respective replies.

"So, if I understand this deployment you are asking for correctly, you want to go to the Geyser system on the East side of Tarren, looking for…?" He trailed off, looking at the camera.

"We believe the source of these Double Users has something to do with these geysers, sir. I know that a lot of the traffic we've had has been in the central region, where we are stationed, but we believe the geysers out East hold some sort of key to rooting out these Double Users," Sergeant Vander Esch said.

"Ah, I see. Well, it would be excellent to find their source, but what do you plan on doing then? If we find a horde of Wild Ones out there somewhere, it will take a full-scale invasion to capture or kill them all. Two squadrons wouldn't do anything to a large group," Chancellor Ambrose said.

"Sir, this is less about Wild Ones and more about the Red Hand. If we can find out where they're coming from, we can possibly capture them and end the chaos they've been creating," Vander Esch replied.

"Ah, those anarchists… good. If you can find them, capture them and bring them all to Rotun. The MSF can handle them from there," Chancellor Ambrose said. Sergeant Vander Esch nodded before replying.

"Of course, sir. If we can find them, we'll apprehend them immediately," He said.

"Alright… well, it will take about a week, but I'll send a second unit to assist you in your search, and then a plane to take you all," Chancellor Ambrose said.

"Couldn't Sergeant Vander Esch just open a portal for us?" Clay asked.

"The Sergeant's portals can only open in spots he can see at the moment or places he's familiar with. He could open one from there back here, but not here to there," Vincent said, Clay nodding in acknowledgment of the answer.

"If I may ask, Sergeant Vander Esch, how did your squad come across this information?," Chancellor Ambrose asked, a bit of suspicion in his voice.

Vander Esch hesitated before he replied.

"While fighting a Double User, he mentioned them. Said it had been hell ever since he woke up near them," Vander Esch said, making Clay and Albert look at one another for a moment.

"Ah… alright then. I suppose that's as good a lead as you've had in a while regarding them. Good luck, then, Titan Squad," The Chancellor said before disconnecting.

"God, I hate talking to him…" Vincent said, sighing in relief.

"Hey, at least you didn't call me 'Adam' in front of him again," Vander Esch chuckled.

Clay listened as the two heckled each other…

"And what does he think we'll find there, anyways? 'Horde of Wild Ones' what, does he think we'll just stumble upon King Ichabod?"

Clay's memory sprang to life, and in just that moment, he stood up, slamming his hand on the table, bringing silence to the room.

"Ichabod…" Clay said, looking at Vincent.

"I remember, when our father died… he told me something. His dying wish was for me to 'find Ichabod'… who is that?" Clay asked.

The room was dead silent for a solid 10 seconds before Julie finally spoke up.

"Clay… um… Ichabod is, er, was…" she stuttered.

"Ichabod was the king of Clemence during their reign over the world," Adam said.

"Yeah… he's been dead for nearly 80 years now…" Vincent said.

Clay's shoulders dropped in realization as he began to slowly sit back down.

"Sorry… I don't know what came over me. I just heard that name and remembered what he said," Clay said, holding his head in his hands for a minute, trying to calm down. Albert stared at him for a moment before looking down a second, getting up to leave another second later.

"Alright, let's get our business here taken care of. I'll get a schedule ready. We'll move out for the geysers in one week," Adam said. He and Vincent left while Julie patted Clay on the shoulder.

"Hey Clay, want to help me around the lab a bit?" She asked. Clay nodded, standing and looking back to Albert for just a moment as he went to the two brothers' room.

Albert entered his room and went to his trunk, opening it and digging through it before pulling out a leather briefcase with the name "Rick B" embroidered on the front.

Albert opened it up, pulling out a set of black and white photos of a man in a military uniform, one of which the man was standing in front of a throne.

"What were you trying to tell us?" Albert asked no one, pulling out a paper from the bag.

The paper was written in a strange language Albert had looked at before but never understood. He pulled up a translation app on his phone, changing the translated language to "Clemencian" and brought his camera up to the paper.

"FOR OFFICIAL USE ONLY"

"Field Report: Arnold Lewis, December 5, 1941,"

Albert shook his head as he looked over the writing on the paper, looking back to the photos a second before continuing reading.

"I have successfully detained the rebel cell. Their powers were mostly untrained, and therefore were easy to suppress. I am soon putting in a request for leave so that I may visit my wife and daughter in the South. I wish to prepare them for our Exodus, King Ichabod,"

Albert's brow furrowed as he read the last sentence again.

"So he did work under Ichabod… but what Exodus?" Albert asked, looking through the bag a bit more, only finding a single other paper, folded and kept in a small pocket.

Translating it, Albert read again.

"Arnold, my love, Agnes and I eagerly await your return. We are hoping we can set out soon to escape Clemence before the Exodus, but I don't want to leave without you. I believe Agnes' powers are starting to develop, and she will need to have someone in her life to be a father to her and train her to use her ability properly. Manipulation magic like this is extremely powerful, from what I've read, and I don't want her hurting anyone because she doesn't know her own strength,"

Albert sat back, sighing as he read the letter over and over.

"You never did like to show the whole picture, dad…" Albert said, frustration in his voice as he put everything back again.

He pulled his phone out just a moment after, going back to the search bar.

"Clemence Exodus"

No relevant results…

"Magic-User Exodus"

No relevant results…

"Arnold Lewis"

No relevant results….

Albert sighed in frustration, staring at the black bar flashing on the search engine's text box.

"King Ichabod"

Julie and Clay stopped by Julie's room, a mess of trash and randomly assorted items strewn throughout the room. In the corner of a room was a 5-gallon bucket full of dirt.

"So, I dunno if you heard, but the report on you guys' family came back," Julie said, grabbing the bucket and pouring it out onto the floor, much to Clay's confusion.

"No, I don't think I heard…" he said, staring at the pile of dirt she dumped on her floor before she knelt down, touching it and letting two dirt men rise from it, each of them about 4 feet tall.

"You two, clean up this place, please," She said to the dirt men, prompting them both to begin picking up trash, organizing her personal items, and cleaning the room as she approached Clay again.

"Well, the MSF looked through your family history, but didn't find much. Your Grandmother, Agnes, married Aaron Barrett, but we don't know anything more than that. Funny enough, they couldn't even track down your grandmother's Maiden name. It's like she didn't exist until she married Aaron," Julie said, shrugging. Clay thought for a moment, looking down with his brow furrowing.

"Honestly, I don't remember much about my Grandmother on dad's side. She never talked much, but she seemed happy with her life. I never heard about anything to do with Magic Users around her. It was kind of a taboo topic in her house, like with a lot of them these days," Clay said.

"Well, we might just have to pay her a visit after the geyser trip. Maybe we'll get some sort of insight into how you guys ended up with Mana in your veins?" Julie shrugged, chuckling. Clay rubbed his neck, laughing a bit, before noticing the dirt men were already nearly finished.

"Wow, those guys work fast," He said, Julie turning back to the room, which was nearly spotless.

"Good work, fellas! You never let me down," She said, smiling as she pulled the bucket to the middle of the room, letting both of them step inside and return to their original pile form.

"Guess your power comes in handy pretty often," Clay said as Julie returned the bucket to a corner of the room near the door. She walked over to him, shrugging and crossing her arms.

"Not as much in combat, since the guys are a bit lacking in the whole 'intelligence' thing, but it's pretty versatile," Julie said.

"Hey, I know this seems a bit out of the blue, but I want you to know how much I appreciate your help with trying to save these Double Users," Julie said, "I know that some of the squad here would just prefer to kill them and be done with it. But you, me, and Adam, to an extent, all know that Double Users aren't just evil like the news and Chancellor Ambrose claims. Just… Thank you for giving them a chance," She said. Clay was caught off guard by her words, but after a moment, he figured out what to say in reply.

"Well, just like you asked us when we arrived in Titan squad, I originally joined just for revenge on Magic Users. They killed both of my parents. When I signed up, I wanted to take the fight to them. But seeing all of you in action, meeting Carter, and figuring out Albert and I were Magic Users too… I guess I just had a change in perspective," Clay said, looking down.

"I signed up thinking Magic Users were some sort of virus, just like everyone else. But now I see we're just people, and like people, there's a lot of good and bad ones," Clay said. Julie smiled, stepping forward and throwing her arms around Clay. Though he was a bit surprised, he hugged her back, sighing.

"Look, Clay, after all this is over, all the fighting. Do you know what you want to do?" Julie asked, still hugging him.

"I dunno… if we beat the Red Hand, and help all the Double Users, then I'd probably just want to find a home. Somewhere to settle into and rest for a while," Clay said. Julie nodded, her chin bumping his shoulder lightly with her nods.

"That sounds nice," She said, slowly pulling herself back and looking into his eyes. Clay returned the gaze, both of them getting lost in each other's sight. They slowly moved closer, their eyes moving to one another's mouths. Clay's heart began pumping rapidly, adrenaline shooting through his system at the moment Julie ran her hand down to touch his hand.

But out of the corner of her eye, Julie saw a dirt man standing in the bucket.

Julie screamed and jumped back, causing Clay to step back, yelping himself as the dirt man fell back into the bucket again.

"I… I didn't do that," Julie said, pointing to the bucket, her hand shaking. Clay looked at her hand, then his own, for just a second, obviously just as confused as she was.

One week after the request was accepted, the plane arrived on time, with Titan squad boarding alone.

"Where's the secondary squad?" Albert asked. The pilot who was preparing for the takeoff looked back as they all got into their seats.

"We'll be stopping to pick them up and fuel up. It's a bit of a long trip," He said. Albert nodded and sat back. Adam looked to make sure everyone was strapped in before sitting down.

The pilot shut the door between the cockpit and the cargo hold, where they all sat. The plane was a small cargo transport, with seats on either side of the cargo hold and a large, open area wide enough for a couple of vehicles before the back loading ramp came up and connected to the tail.

"Julie, did you find anything in your research this morning about Exitium?" Adam asked.

"Not much; most of it was just ghost stories about some demon with the same name. He had no record in our logs; without his last name, this "Lance" can't really be looked up either. There are a hundred different guys in our wanted registry with the same name. But, I didn't have time to filter by ability, so when we land, I might have time to find more on him," Julie said. Adam nodded, closing his eyes to think.

"And what about the geysers?" Adam asked Julie.

"Well, they're definitely strange in the context of most geysers in the world, but they're not suspicious, for the most part. They span along the Eastern edge of both Tarren and Brakata and hook through the center of Brakata. All I could find was that they emit a mix of steam, Methane, and Carbon dioxide, and they pump so much out of the underbelly of the Earth's crust that a lot of them tend to suck in air from time to time to replace the space that the other gasses leave when they flow out," She said. Adam nodded, sighing at the lack of information.

"Titan squad… listen up," Adam said as the plane ran down the runway outside the HQ and pulled up, into the air. Titan squad looked to him, all of them feeling the pressure from the ascent but focused on Adam.

"I talked to the Chancellor again, and I believe we need to watch our backs during this expedition. He tried to talk me out of this expedition, claiming us capturing the Double Users and sending them to the Capital is enough out of us," Adam explained. Albert and Vincent both furrowed their brows as Clay spoke up.

"What about all the knowledge we got from Carter? Doesn't that have to mean something?" He asked.

Adam nodded, bringing a hand up to his chin.

"For us, it absolutely does. But the Chancellor doesn't know that we capture and keep Double Users. Technically, our assignment is to send any and all that we capture to the Capital. That's why the elevator doesn't lead to Julie's lab. If he comes to inspect our facilities and sees it, he may shut down our operation," Adam said.

"Do we have any idea what's even happening to them at the Capital?" Julie asked.

"Not exactly… but it can't be good. Once they enter, they never leave, so they're obviously being killed… but if that's all they wanted, they would just order us to kill on sight. They're doing something to these Double Users… but I don't think we'll have a chance to find out, for the moment, at least. I'm not sure what it was about the Chancellor's tone, but I have a feeling he's planning on pulling the plug on Titan Squad. Between the suspicion in his tone during our conference call, and his tone this morning, I believe if we're not careful, we may find out sooner than later what happens to Magic Users that are brought to the Capital," Adam said, crossing his arms.

The plane flew high over plains and farmland, clusters of trees scattered throughout the land as they made their way West.

"Agh… I need a haircut soon…," Adam said, running his hand through the longer hair on top of his head.

Julie chuckled, letting her hair down from her usual bun, dropping it down past her shoulder blades.

"I could use a trim too. Hate when some parts of my hair grow faster than others," She said.

Adam looked over to Albert, giving him an upnod.

"Albert, your hair is getting fairly long, too. We may not be expected to keep our hair in regulation, but think you might need a trim soon? It's almost over your eyes," Adam said.

Albert looked down, noticing he could see his hair out of the corners of his eyes.

"I can pull it back, if nothing else. I've always worn it long, except for when we went into basic and were forced to cut it," He said. Adam shrugged, Julie looking at Clay.

"It's not fair that we can't rag on you about your hair too, Mr. Spiffy," Julie joked.

"I think you just did rag on me about it," Clay said, causing himself, Albert, and Adam to all laugh while Vincent dozed off in his seat.

As the plane continued West, dark clouds began rolling slightly above the plane. The plane soared into the rain ahead, thunder booming not too far from the carrier.

The pilot was trying to keep control of the plane when a single lightning bolt shot into the plane, ripping the edge of the left wing off.

Adam stood, looking outside before looking to the cockpit. The pilot was still struggling to keep them balanced as he set the plane to descend.

Another bolt of lightning struck the cockpit, ripping a hole in it right behind the pilot's seat, his weight pushing him back into it.

"We have a situation! Julie, come with me, everyone else, get unbuckled and await my order," Adam said. Julie immediately got up and ran over as Vander Esch opened a portal to the cockpit, and the two of them stepped through it, looking down at the hole. Vander Esch squatted down to try and grab the pilot while Julie took to the controls, struggling to pull up.

"Adam, this thing is on auto-pilot!" She said while everyone else was getting up. Albert woke Vincent up so he could join them as well.

Adam looked under the plane to see the seat had fallen off the plane's bottom.

"Alright, I have an idea. Everyone get in the cockpit!" Adam ordered, prompting Clay, Albert and Vincent to step through the portal.

Adam closed the portal to the cargo hold, looking out the windshield of the plane.

"Alright, we're gonna carry some momentum, but this is our only shot," He said, opening a portal off to the side of the windshield where he could barely see through the rain before opening another behind them.

"Get through, now!" Adam yelled. Everyone jumped through the portal onto the wet grass, looking back once they stood at the plane soaring towards the ground. Adam ordered everyone into a cluster of trees as they watched the plane crash down into the earth. The plane was ripped to shreds, skidding along the ground while it was ripped apart by the force in which it landed. Titan Squad watched as a group of black Humvees approached the wreckage, each unloading a group of 4 soldiers who began scanning the wreckage, rifles at the ready.

"What the hell happened...?" Albert asked.

"I'm not sure... it seemed to be weather, but that seemed a bit precise to just be the storm..," Vander Esch said, shaking his head.

"Let's rendezvous with the squad down there, see if we can figure out what happened and what to do next," Vander Esch said.

He opened a portal and the squad passed through, the soldiers looking up and seeing them, immediately lowering their weapons.

"Titan Squad. What happened here?" Asked Bullpup, who was in command of the squad that arrived at the crash. All 12 soldiers stopped to address them, saluting for a second before continuing their search, all but Bullpup, who spoke with Adam. The two of them had to almost shout as the rain and thunder continued around them.

"The storm gave us some turbulence, but lightning struck the cockpit and killed our pilot. We used my power to escape before the plane crashed down," Sergeant Vander Esch explained. Bullpup nodded, pointing out West towards a set of mountains.

"We had reports of Red Hand members out in the mountains, but once we saw the bird going down, we stopped to help," Bullpup said.

"Then this crash was probably intentional. Where's the nearest base?" Adam asked.

"We came from Rotun, about 50 miles East. But we brought enough manpower to combat most anything they have. Now, with you guys, we shouldn't have any issue taking them down," Bullpup replied.

Adam looked back to the mountains, his eyes narrowing.

"Do we have any idea how many there are?" He asked.

"Reports say five, sir," Bullpup replied. Adam crossed his arms, his brow furrowing.

"…fine. We'll do some recon, see what the situation is, and go from there. I don't want to risk lives without being properly informed, but these days we're used to a lack of information, aren't we?" Adam said. Bullpup only chuckled, putting his hands on his hips.

"That's all it's been since Clemence, sir," He said, sighing.

Another 2 Humvees were requested on-site to transport Titan Squad, and as they packed in, they rode with the rest of the soldiers towards the mountains to investigate the reports that Bullpup and his squad received. The vehicles drove up the winding roads to the top of one of the mountains in a small range of them, the squad grabbing binoculars and high magnification handheld optics to survey the area. The visibility on the top of the mountain was better than most areas due to the elevation but was still limited in the rain, and while they searched and looked around, it began to get darker.

"It's been about an hour, and we've found nothing. We need to get back to base before night completely falls," Bullpup said as he approached Adam, who had a pair of binoculars in his hands.

"Alright… I suppose the storm was natural. Still, I have a feeling we're close to the enemy…" he said, lowering the binoculars and looking back to Bullpup.

"Well, we can come back in the morning to try and flush them out and get you guys to your destination before the crash. But we need to get back to base soon," Bullpup said, looking to his men and gesturing for them to pack up.

Adam followed him back to the Humvees as Titan Squad packed up the ocular equipment with the rest of the men. Most of them seemed fairly normal working with them.

"Have these guys worked with you before?" Albert whispered to Vincent as they put a couple of sets of binoculars back into their spots in the trunk of a Humvee.

"Yeah, Bullpup and Sergeant Vander Esch have worked together on several missions. Funny enough, these guys are the most open-minded ones we've worked with. Most squads don't take kindly to us just because we're Magic Users," Vincent replied. Albert looked down for just a second before continuing to put the gear away.

Julie struggled to move a box in another Humvee truck aside so she could put a tripod back, but to no avail. With a huff, Julie pulled the box out, stumbling backward before Clay caught her by the arms, stopping her from falling.

"Oh! Clay… thanks," Julie said, setting the box down. Clay nodded, rubbing his neck a bit. Both of them were a bit red, Julie looking down to avoid eye contact for a second with Clay.

"This stuff never goes in the way it came out, y'know?" He said, both of them chuckling. Julie touched the ground, bringing up a group of three earthen men who she commanded to organize the gear again. They immediately began moving boxes and bags, getting it all into the trunk while Clay and Julie helped others pack up without another word to one another.

Soon enough, the Humvees were ready to move out. Everyone loaded up and rolled down the mountains again, winding down to the base and around once, the soldiers with flashlights looking all over for the Red Hand members while the Humvees entered a small valley between two of the mountains on the range.

"Hold on, stop!" Bullpup yelled from the back of the convoy of Humvees as they rolled to a stop in the road.

"What? What is it?" The driver of the first car called back. Bullpup shone his flashlight ahead of them, past where the headlights reached. Ahead of them, about a quarter-mile ahead, the road was blocked off by a set of rock spires that jutted out of the ground, like stalagmites sticking out of the ground, arranged in a near-wall formation to make it impossible to get through.

"It's the Red Hand! They must be close! Spread out and search, but keep an eye on everyone else, don't get separated!" Bullpup called. Everyone immediately got out of the vehicles, grabbed their rifles, and began to search the area.

Titan Squad split up, each of them searching with a different group of soldiers, with Bullpup and Adam standing by at the vehicles. However, with the rain still pouring down and dusk being replaced by the cowled darkness of night, it seemed that the search would lead nowhere.

"If they don't find anything, what do you think we should do next?" Bullpup asked Adam.

"Well, assuming we aren't engaged, I'd say I can make 2 portals. One up to the top of the spire wall, so I can see to the other side, and the other in front of the vehicles to get them to the other side, big enough that we can drive through," Adam said, crossing his arms as he looked back to the wall of rocky spires.

"You still aren't used to portals that big. Think you can handle it for long enough for us to pass through?" Bullpup asked.

"I'll be fine. It's only fatigue. It's fine," He replied, looking back to the valley as the soldiers reached the edge of a forest, now using flashlights to look up the mountains and through the trees without anyone entering the woods.

"That's enough. Come on back," Bullpup said in his communicator to the rest of the squad.

Adam looked at the top of the wall as he and Bullpup both heard a rumbling noise, like the Earth moving.

Suddenly, a spire shot out from the side of one of the mountains that Adam and Bullpup faced, forcing the two of them to split and jump to opposite sides, Adam towards the soldiers and Bullpup jumping towards the spire wall. The rock weapon shot like a spear into the side of the Humvee they were beside, stabbing through the vehicle's armor and pushing so far into it that the tip of the spire broke through the window on the other side.

As the soldiers looked back at what had happened to their commanders, the tree line of the forest they faced burst into flames, the heat suddenly hitting the men and forcing them away from the tree line.

Bullpup looked up the wall as a Silhouette stood on top of the spires, looking up as the rain faded away, giving some visibility back to the soldiers, and most likely, to the enemy as well.

The soldiers slowly stepped back, Albert and Vincent staying with them while Julie got back to Adam, making sure he was alright before she summoned a few dirt men from the mountain.

"C'mon, find the enemy, guys..." she whispered, Clay trying to see, from where he and the other two were, the location of any of the attackers.

"Hey, there!" Clay motioned to Julie to look, and as she did, he pointed out a female silhouette standing about halfway up the mountain. As they took note of her, she sent a rock spire into a dirt man's chest.

"We have a Mike Uniform on top of the spires in front... no movement, but I think it's elemental," Bullpup said through his communicator, Clay grabbing his own to reply.

"Got a female one up the mountain to the South; pretty sure it was the one that blocked our path," Clay said. Julie summoned four more dirt men to move towards the woman.

Three of the soldiers looked over and took aim at the woman up the mountain, watching her as she walked to the side, vanishing into a cloud of smoke and ash.

"A Double User?" Clay said, his brow furrowing as he thought over what happened, looking at the man standing on the wall. He jumped backward off the wall, the same cloud making him disappear behind the wall. Bullpup and Clay barely saw it in between the spires. Julie got rid of her men, then looked over as Clay thought over the situation.

"No… they have a Magic-User with power like Adam's," Clay said. He practically froze, analyzing the situation before he came up with a conclusive idea of what the Red Hand was actually there to do.

As he thought, the flames along the tree line died down just as fast as they appeared, leaving only a line-wide enough to remain a barrier but low enough not to illuminate the area.

Above them, clouds were concentrated in the sky to cover the sunset over the valley, rendering the entire valley in complete darkness, with no sun or moonlight to give the soldiers any sort of vision.

In the trees, Vin Vale stood observing what he could past the wall of flames. His outfit was of an older design, a thick, green button-up shirt with the long sleeves rolled up to his elbows, pockets on either side, a black leather belt around his midriff, pants of similar material and color, and black laced boots that came up above the ankles. Beside him, Lupos wore the same, both of them standing on the larger of the branches, unable to see the movements of the soldiers, but keeping watch for attacks.

"We taking prisoners today?" Lupos asked, looking to Vale, whose almost lifeless eyes stared ahead at the scene behind the fire.

"If Lewis' descendants are here… no. If Exitium gets them, or they figure out how their powers really work, as Lewis did…, we'd stand no chance against them. Better to take them out before they can use their real powers against us," Vale said.

"Hell, it didn't seem like their dad even knew what he had," Lupos said, "and considering Tarren doesn't take kindly to our people, if they're even still alive, I doubt they'll have a chance to-" Lupos replied, Vale interrupting him.

"**I said**, we're killing them if they're here. No matter what, I don't want them being brought back to the Ark," Vale replied emphatically. Lupos looked at him for a moment before his eyes darted to the ground.

"Alright… I'll make sure to keep an eye out. But do you really think they're that much of a threat?" Lupos asked.

"They're not already in the Ark, even though Exitium and his little helper both found them two different times… they're absolutely a threat," Vale said, "Get Carmen ready. I'll have Chris send Ruby back to hit them again from the side, turn their attention away from you two. And remember not to get snatched up. If those Lewis kids have a grip on you, Chris won't be able to get you out,"

Clay yelled to the soldiers, calling them over. While they kept a decent space between them all, Bullpup ducked underneath the spire, and soon, they were all within hearing distance of Clay.

"They're using Guerrilla tactics. I think I can plot their moves before they make them. We just have to know how to react," Clay said.

"So, most likely, they'll aim for leadership first, and try to scramble us and pick us off one by one," Adam replied, still looking around for sight of the enemy from beside the rock spire that had slammed into his humvee.

"Exactly. But I don't think they actually know too much about our ranks if this is what they're doing. So, we have one of our ground troops giving commands listed to him and try to draw them out using him as bait," Clay replied.

"The only issue is finding out where they're going to attack from," Bullpup replied, kneeling down. He took off his ballistic mask, showing his dark skin and brown eyes.

"Here's my theory for that," Clay said, looking to the forest.

"Along the mountains, there's not many places to hide. They could have the high ground, but it doesn't seem like they have many weapons besides their powers, which we already know three of. So, if we watch the mountains with two men to call out if they see the one making these rock spires, and one more watching the other side of the spire wall to find the one keeping us in the dark, we might be able to take them down and give ourselves an advantage," Clay said.

"Alright… then we'll make a couple of sets of commands for one of our soldiers, but what if we need to change plans? We can't communicate the change without giving away Bullpup and myself," Vander Esch said, thinking, "Unless, we could set up some sort of code. How about, you hear one of us yell one, it means regroup, two means to engage, then a direction to look on the clock," Adam said.

"Alright, then we have a plan for the soldiers. What about you guys? You aren't exactly equipped like us," Bullpup replied.

"I have a plan for all of us. We just need to set one more command. Also, Vincent, you need to get changed,"

Along the mountain to the South, Ruby Ellifrits, one of the Red Hand's most skilled enforcers, appeared from a plume of smoke. Her blonde hair was tied up in a messy bun. Her pale skin was covered up by a black long-sleeved button-up and a metal-plated chest piece that hugged her stomach and torso. She also wore black cargo pants, with a belt that held several pockets along it, plus an old-looking handheld radio

"Vin, I'm in position. Terra, are you ready?" She said into the radio, squinting to try and look around the valley to see the soldiers.

"Yep, got the vehicles in my sights. Setting the clock to ten seconds, aiming at the front one," Terra replied over the radio, her voice grizzled and made her battle experience apparent.

"Got it, I'll take the second one. Once they have their backs turned, we'll send in Lupos and Sanchez," Ruby replied, barely able to see the soldiers walking back towards the fire barrier.

"The foot soldiers are approaching the forest, but I don't see Titan squad anywhere," Terra said over the radio.

"Me either. They must either be under the vehicles or using my first attack for cover. Your call, do we hit the vehicles in front or try to take them down and draw their attention to us instead?" Ruby asked.

"Hold on," Was her only reply from Terra.

Ruby turned her attention to the soldiers on the ground, hearing one of them yelling instructions and seeing him doing hand motions in the middle of the group. She also noticed another soldier carrying a riot shield with him, while the rest held only their rifles.

"Think we can take out their commander and disorganize them?" Ruby asked.

"Only one way to find out. On three. One, two…"

Ruby looked to the mountains, found a set of rocks near the bottom, and put her hand out towards them.

"Three o'clock!"

From the other side of the mountain, an arrow shot towards the man who was giving instructions, only for the man holding the riot shield to jump in the way, taking the arrow. On the other side of the mountain, Ruby sent a rock spire towards the group, sending it through the chest of one of the men and sending him to the ground.

The man with the Riot shield stood straight before the arrow embedded in his shield exploded, knocking him back and causing the shield to dissipate.

"Hey, that was one of Titan squad's men!" Terra said on the radio.

"Got him. I'll try to take him out," Ruby said. She looked around for another spot to create a spire from, putting her hand out before she noticed the soldiers headed in her direction.

"Oh, shit," She whispered, grabbing her radio.

"Chris, I need an escape here!" She said into the radio.

"We're a bit busy right now, there's guys coming out of the trees everywhere!" A male voice came through the radio.

"Guys?! Did they ambush you? I haven't seen anyone go past the firewall," Ruby said, backing up from her position as the soldiers followed the spire she sent out, up the mountain.

"No, they're not soldiers. They're made from dirt. I think one of those Titan squad guys has some sort of summoning power. They're just standing around, though. They don't seem to be a threat, just yet…," He replied.

Ruby cursed under her breath and began moving along the mountain towards the forest again, radioing to Terra.

"Terra, I need a distraction," She said.

"Hold on. I'm tracking movement in one of the vehicles. I think they're sending someone to make a run for it!"

Just as she said that, Ruby saw the back vehicle's tires screech and send it flying backward, past the fire and into the forest, out of sight as it passed into the trees.

"Shit! Terra, we have a runner!" Ruby said into her radio, seeing another arrow fly off into the forest.

"I couldn't hit it in time… Chris, can you do anything about it?" Terra's voice came through.

Right about that time, a loud crash echoed through the valley.

"The humvee wrecked into the tree. Vin and I are moving in now. Lupos, Sanchez,help us out here if Titan squad is here. Ellifrits, Haney, keep the soldiers busy," Chris' voice replied. Ruby turned her head to the valley again, the soldiers still moving towards her.

"Four," Terra's voice spoke through the radio.

An arrow flew into the ground below the soldiers, who all looked to it, backing up and looking towards the other side of the valley.

"Contact, nine-"

The arrow exploded, sending two of the men flying away in a couple of pieces, the explosion searing their body armor and pushing them about 10 feet away from the arrow.

Three of the men got up, aiming their rifles towards Ruby before she threw her hand to the side, a set of three rock spires firing out from the original one stabbed into the chests of the soldiers. Blood covered the tips of the spires and began pooling around the grass below them.

Ruby was about to run when the sound of a gunshot rang out, and an intense pain shocked her, coming from her shoulder. She fell to the ground, looking back and seeing one of the men aiming their rifle at her, the barrel smoking.

Two others ran at her, holding her to the ground and quickly slapping a dampener to her upper arm. Ruby struggled, trying to listen for something, anything, that could save her.

"Hey, there's nobody here! What the hell?" Chris said into the radio.

A flare then shot into the air, bathing the forest and valley in red light. "Move, move!"

Albert, Julie and Adam ran into the forest from underneath the other Humvees. The earth figures began pointing towards Vin Vale and Chris, Adam looking back just as Terra was pulling her bow back to fire another arrow.

A portal opened right beside Terra, Clay jumping through and pushing her bow to the side.

Terra stepped back, Clay now facing off with her. As Terra lunged forward, Parks' words ran through his head again.

"The trick is to always use their momentum against them. If they lunge forward, sidestep and push them further forward,"

He grabbed her wrist and side-stepped, letting her momentum carry her forward. He stepped behind her and pushed her further forward, putting her off balance and shoving her to the ground, one hand behind her back in Clay's grasp as she fell on her front. Clay grabbed her other wrist, pulling them together and holding her.

Clay let her struggle until she gave out, and once she was tired, he held her wrists with one hand while he pulled out a dampener with the other, attaching it to her shoulder.

Albert, Adam and Julie ran towards the direction the Earthen people pointed, seeing Chris and Vale standing beside the humvee, both of them looking back in shock.

Albert locked eyes with Vale, frozen for just a moment before his hand slowly moved to his hip, and the 1911 he held.

Vin looked to Chris before looking back at the three before them.

"Go!" Julie said, the earthen figures running at them. Albert turned to Chris, seeing him make a fist and Vale vanish into a cloud of smoke. Albert ran forward, pulling out his gun and firing a round straight into Chris' left thigh.

The young Magic Users dropped to a knee, yelling in pain and clutching his leg. The dirt figures grabbed him before Albert reached him, putting a dampener on his neck.

"Where did you send him?" Albert asked, bringing his pistol up and shoving the barrel just below his chin. Chris winced, looking Albert in the eyes.

"Go to hell…" he said. Julie gave the earth men a pair of handcuffs, and they clasped them around Chris' wrists while Julie knelt down to tend to his knee. Albert sighed, turning away and looking back up to the sides of the mountains, towards the other soldiers.

They also sat Ruby up and tended to her wound after cuffing her wrists. The soldiers got ready to bring her down the mountain, before one of them yelled.

"Contact close!"

Just as he raised his rifle, a claw stabbed through his stomach, lifting him off his feet. Lupos used the man as a shield, pushing forward and throwing the body into one of the seven other men who surrounded Ruby. He grabbed the third's rifle, pulling him in front of Lupos just as a bullet fired, zipping past the two of them as Lupos stabbed the third man in the back. He took his rifle, firing on the other men, one of them taking two shots to the back while the last three soldiers got back behind the cover of Ruby's first rock spire she had sent at the Humvee.

Before the men had a chance to move in on Lupos, another figure appeared from the trees. A dark-haired woman, her arms coated with a glossy metal substance. She wore an outfit similar to Ruby's, with her sleeves rolled up to expose her arms more. She ran forward, pulling one hand back to strike, but as she swung, her target brought a hand up, and a riot shield materialized around it, blocking the strike.

Sanchez tried to swing with her other arm, but Vincent swung his arm to match her's, the side of his shield striking the inside of her elbow.

Vincent and Sanchez both kept moving, swing after swing. They attempted and blocked, trying to gain an edge. Finally, while he blocked, Vincent pulled a pistol from his hip and drove himself forward, face to face with Sanchez as he put the barrel of the gun to her stomach, firing off three rounds.

Sanchez fell backward. Vincent looked down at the girl before noticing there was no blood coming from where he shot. Kneeling down, he pulled her shirt up, seeing her stomach had been coated with the same metal as her arms. He looked up into her eyes as she swung again, landing a punch straight into his jaw, sending him to the side, knocking him unconscious. She stayed on her back, holding her stomach while pulling her shirt down.

"Pervert…" she said, lying back and catching her breath, the bullets not wounding but obviously still hitting her with the same force. The soldiers surrounded her before one of them was shot by Lupos, all of them but one turning their attention to him while the one moved to help Vincent.

"Give us some cover while we wait for Chris! Vale will help him while Charles gets Terra, and we're getting out of here," Lupos said. Ruby looked up to a cliff side above them, sending a large rock spire along the mountain for them to stay behind while they waited for Chris to exfiltrate them.

Albert saw the fight, looking back at the crashed Humvee in the trees.

"Hey, something happening at-," he said, everyone looking at him as he watched Vale jump down from one of the trees behind Chris. Albert's eyes widened as he pointed to Vale, yelling.

"Hey!" He yelled, pulling out his pistol as the rest of the team there turned back to the two.

Vale pulled Chris' dampener out, the earth-men turning to him and pushing Vale back as Chris transported himself away.

The black hair, the anger in his eyes... Albert realized the second he saw Vale that it was the same pyrokinetic that his father had saved him from, who was with Lupos when his mother was killed. He was the one who burned the store down.

Albert ran at Vale while putting away his gun and, seeing he wasn't being transported yet, tackled Vale to the ground, the dirt men turning again to spectators in the fight. Vale struggled to push Albert away before he grabbed Vale's throat, bringing his arm back and sending a fist into his cheekbone. Vale brought his arms up to protect himself, and Albert raised up again, another punch driving into his stomach, knocking the wind out of him. Albert looked into the eyes of Vale, panting while Julie and Adam approached from behind him. The line of fire at the edge of the forest faded out as Albert held Vale down.

Albert pulled his combat knife from his boot, bringing it to Vale's throat just underneath where he held it. Adam and Julie came closer, circling around the two of them.

"Albert, wait," Adam said.

"This is it, our chance to end this," Albert replied, pressing the edge of the blade into Vale's throat. He grunted in pain and looked up to the other two members of Titan squad, who stood back but pleaded with Albert.

"If we can find where they're coming from, we can take them all down, not just one person! He holds the key to all this, Albert!" Julie yelled, looking back for a second to the rest of the battle.

"We could capture any of them, and they'd probably know what he does!" Albert yelled back, keeping the blade firmly pressed against the Pyrokinetic's windpipe.

"We don't know the next time we'll be able to capture any of them! Do you know how long we've been chasing them?!" Adam yelled.

"And how many times have they attacked this squad, specifically? They did it this time. They'll do it again," Albert replied. He looked up as two dirt men rose up, pulling his arm away from Vale's throat. Julie ran up, putting a dampener on him before he could act or be transported, and she and Adam restrained him.

Albert struggled against the dirt men, finally stepping backward while Vale was restrained. He looked up to the trees for just a moment, seeing a rustling in the branches. Albert pulled out his pistol, training it up into the branches as he watched several branches suddenly shake in a trail that led away from him and the rest of the squad towards the mountains where the soldiers were retreating to tend to their wounded.

"Looks like they're retreating. Good riddance," Albert said, slowly putting his gun away and pulling out his radio.

"Clay, are you alright? Did you get the one shooting those arrows?" He asked.

Clay was standing with a foot firmly but calmly pressing on the lower back of the woman, just above her cuffed arms.

"Yeah, I got her. I think there's just one left we haven't engaged yet," Clay replied.

"Who's that?" Albert asked.

"The one who caused the clouds. I think they're the one who killed the pilot and made us crash. I think it's their scout since all we've seen from it was when it looked us over from the rock spire wall,"

Just as he said this, the wind began to pick up, thunder in the distance an ominous signal of the situation.

A plume of smoke appeared in front of Clay and Terra, and a man dressed in the same green fatigues as Vale and Lupos stepped towards the two of them, with a Luger pistol in his hand.

"Dammit, I hate being right…," Clay said, putting his radio away and raising his hands.

"I don't suppose we could talk about this?" Clay asked, chuckling nervously as the weather manipulator stepped forward, pulling the dampener off of Terra while keeping the weapon trained on Clay.

"Chris, it's time we exfiltrate," He said into his own radio, Clay slowly backing up as he spoke, Terra sitting up and huffing in frustration.

"What about Vin?" Chris's voice replied.

"He got unlucky. With all of Titan Squad here, we can't risk more of us getting captured," The man said.

"And who allowed you to make that decision?" The voice replied, a third interrupting them, the voice of Lupos.

"Chris, get us out of here, now. We'll figure something out,"

Charles nodded before Ruby's shaken voice came over the radio.

"We're not leaving here until we kill at least one of them!"

From the other side of the mountain, Albert saw a rock spire fire from a cliff face, moving with lightning speed towards Clay.

Albert's adrenaline rushed, his head pounded, and his heart started to beat out of his chest. Albert's instincts took him over, and as he put his hand out towards the rock spire, his entire body strained, every muscle in him tensing up. He could feel... everything. Every power, and every bit of Mana around him, he felt he could nearly pick apart each power. Yet, for now, he focused on one. He felt his mind embrace the feeling of rock like he held a sword of stone in his hand.

Then he swung...

Chapter 5

✦✦✦✦✦✦

"**A**rnold Lewis? I heard the name in one of Julie's usual rants about Double Users, but I don't know too much about him," Vincent stated.

He and Albert sat in the command center with the sunset long passed and the rest of the squad in their beds. The lights were off, but the computers in the room gave a low, blue illumination to the surroundings.

"Gotcha... look, this is something I want to trust you with, but you have to promise me you won't tell anyone else, not Sergeant Vander Esch, not Clay, nobody. Alright?" Albert requested, leaning forward in his black computer chair across from Vincent's.

"Why the secrecy? I mean, we all keep enough secrets from Ambrose, but not usually from the rest of the squad," Vincent replied, crossing his arms in his seat.

"This isn't something I want Clay pursuing. If he gets it in his head that I'm right about this, he'll try to follow me in training," Albert shared, resting his elbows on his knees and interlocking his fingers.

"And what's so bad about that?" Vincent asked.

"He's on the front lines enough as it is, on this squad with us. He's got a good head on his shoulders, but when he's faced with people who won't hesitate to kill him, I don't know if he'll do the same to them," Albert explained.

"Alright, I guess I can get behind that... so, what's this secret, first of all?" Vincent asked.

"I don't think our power is what the government, the military, or anyone thinks it is," Albert said. He pulled the letter and pictures from his pocket he had found in the briefcase.

"When my father died, he left me a briefcase, one that Clay doesn't know about. Inside, there were all these pictures and letters around someone named 'Arnold Lewis.'" Albert said, laying them out on Vincent's desk for him to look over.

"Alright, so what… this guy is your ancestor? Why does that make you think your power is different?" Vincent questioned. Albert got on Vincent's computer, looking up pictures of King Ichabod.

"Well, at first, nothing. I thought it was all just for family history. But, I think I put together a piece of the puzzle that the military doesn't know about," Albert replied, clicking on an image and expanding it.

The image was in black and white, of King Ichabod in his throne room, surrounded by a team of advisors and military ranks. They were all older men, besides Ichabod, who looked like he was in his 30's. He was dressed in a darker-colored garment and the crown on his head was covered with differently shaded jewels. The rest of the men wore either white lab coats or traditional military attire, with flat caps and medals on their chests.

"Now, look there," Albert said, zooming in to one of the officers and sliding the picture of Lewis to Vincent to compare.

"Well, I'll be damned…" Vincent said, shaking his head and holding his chin as he leaned back, "But how does that change what power you have?" he asked, looking back to Albert.

"Well, here's the kicker,"Albert began, typing in "Dantalion,"

"I never found anything on an Arnold Lewis from what we know about Clemence. But I looked through the King's Royal guard, and among them, the name 'Dantalion' came up. I looked it up, and…"

Bringing up an online information site about the name, a picture came up, with the same face as the picture he had.

"So Arnold Lewis was a royal guard member named Dantalion, how do-" Vincent began, but Albert interrupted.

"Hold on, hold on… his power is listed here," Albert said, scrolling before stopping on a small info list.

Name: Dantalion

Rank: Ensign

Power: magic Manipulation

Vincent stared at the screen, his mouth agape.

Albert stood up with his arms crossed while he let Vincent process this.

"So, what does this mean? You have this power?" Vincent asked, looking to Albert, obviously still trying to wrap his head around the discovery.

"I do… and I think if we can use the Red Hand's powers against them, they'll be practically easy to stop. From what I've seen and heard during briefings, they don't have too much strategy in how they attack. They're basically terrorists that have destructive powers instead of weapons," Albert said.

"So, why have you and Clay only been able to suppress people's powers before?" Vincent asked.

"I've thought it over in my head, and I think it's because we never trained our abilities. We've only taken them at face value, and I think it may be the same way for all of us. Think about it. Has anyone ever taught you how to use your power?" Albert asked.

"No, everyone in Titan Squad has used our powers out of instinct, as far as I know. For a lot of us, our parents either weren't aware of the power or weren't around to show us," Vincent said, leaning forward again and looking at the floor.

"Look, just let me test something here. May I?" Albert asked, putting a hand above Vincent's shoulder. Upon his nodding, Albert put a hand on his upper arm, just below his sleeve. He then closed his eyes, feeling the power flow up into him from Vincent. His first instinct was to push the feeling away, just as he had always done before, but instead, he reached out, grabbing the power within himself, directing it.

"Spear," Albert spoke.

A gold aura surrounded one of Vincent's hands, and a metal spear manifested within his grasp. Vincent stared down at the spear; his eyes widened. He looked up at Albert, whose eyes were still closed. Vincent smiled, chuckling to himself as he looked back at the spear just as Albert opened his eyes, stepping back and letting go of Vincent, triggering his spear to dissipate.

"That's… that's one hell of an ability you have," Vincent said.

Clay's eyes were tightly closed in anticipation of the rock spire hitting him as he had seen it coming but had no time to react. However, upon opening his eyes, Clay looked towards the spire, and saw the rock had turned mid-motion, avoiding him. Clay followed the spire with his eyes to the end, where he saw Terra, impaled from the back, pinned to another cliff-face. She was off the ground, her head facing up into the sky. A trail of blood ran from her mouth down her cheek, and a lot more blood covered the rock spire and the ground below her from the wound.

The Red Hand's scout backed up, seeing the rock spire, but before he or Clay could do anything more, the man was transported away.

"Ruby, what the hell did you do?!" Lupos yelled at the woman, whose hand was still outstretched and shaking.

"I… I don't know," She said, looking at her hand. Her eyes teared up as she stared at the hand, grabbing her wrist with her other hand.

"What have I done?" she said, her voice choppy and shaken.

"Since when can she turn her spikes like that?" Chris asked, Lupos taking a second look at the spire.

"She can't," Lupos said, looking first to Clay, who was obviously surprised by what happened, then to Albert, at the edge of the forest, who was on his knees, exhausted.

Albert laid down on his back, panting and looking up to the trees and the bits of sky he saw past the branches.

"We're out of time. Get us out of here," Lupos said, looking back to Chris.

With that, the five of them were transported away from the valley, leaving Terra's body and Vin Vale behind with Titan squad.

Between the cleanup of the area, the loss of supplies and men on Tarren's side, and the capture of Vin Vale, Titan Squad was ordered to return to their barracks, pending their first mission failure.

"I don't want the Chancellor to find out we have Vale," Adam said to Bullpup as the soldiers tended to their wounded, and Titan Squad helped out where they could. Albert was laid down near the Humvees, and Clay sat with him until he woke up.

"You're going behind the Chancellor's back again? Why?" Bullpup asked.

"We're learning more and more about the Red Hand, and about magic in general. I believe the more we learn, the more Chancellor Ambrose will want to put a stop to it. I want to find out what Vale knows before the MSF confiscates him from us," Adam said.

"Alright, so what, you'll keep him in your barracks?" Bullpup asked.

"We have a spot for him back home, don't worry," Adam replied, crossing his arms and looking over at the restrained pyrokinetic, and the bandages over his throat.

"Well, as long as that 'spot' is fireproof, I have no objections. This whole thing was you guys' mission anyways," Bullpup replied.

"Not exactly. Our mission was to investigate the geysers out East, but it seems like the Chancellor is cancelling that plan due to the attack," Adam said.

"Well, you know what I mean. Capturing Magic Users is kind of out of my or my men's pay grade. We only tried capturing rocky up there because of your squad," Bullpup replied. Adam nodded, putting a hand on Bullpup's shoulder.

"I appreciate it, James. I hope we can work together again soon," He said.

Bullpup looked back to his squad for a moment, and to the bodies covered by sheets lying in a row.

"No offense to you and your squad, Adam, but I genuinely hope we don't,"

Bullpup walked over to help his squad's injured while Adam looked back to Vale, who sat silently still against a tree.

Vincent and Julie approached, while Adam still thought over their situation.

"I still don't see why we're letting him live. After all the attacks on civilians, the strikes against our men, the overall chaos he's created, he's more trouble than he's worth, if you ask me," Vincent said, standing beside Adam, Julie standing on the other side of him.

"Well, after we question him and get some answers about the Red Hand's origin, he'll definitely face the consequences for his actions. But, I'm glad we got him alive. I don't know how much he'll be willing to tell us, but whatever we can learn from him will be more than what we knew before, at the very least," Julie said.

Vincent shook his head as Adam opened a portal behind Vale into Julie's lab. Her and Vincent pulled Vale through, opening the cell that once held Carter and pushing Vale into it, locking him inside before they passed back through.

The MSF were just beginning to arrive as Albert started to wake up, looking at Clay.

"What happened? Did we find anything out?" He asked, beginning to sit up. Clay threw himself around Albert in a hug, Albert looking at him a moment before returning the hug.

"God, you're alright…" Clay said, relieved.

"Yeah, I'm fine," Albert said with a sigh, "Don't worry, I can't die yet; nobody else would be watching your ass to make sure you aren't killed," Albert chuckled.

"Are you kidding?" Clay said, sitting back up, "If it wasn't for me, you'd have ran off and gotten yourself killed fighting a long time ago,"

"Yeah, sure," Albert replied, rolling his eyes and chuckling as he sat up and scooted back to lean on the side of the Humvee.

"So, what's happening?" he asked.

"We have the Red Hand's leader, but all but one from the rest got away," Clay said.

"What happened to that one?" Albert asked, pointing to the impaled woman.

"I dunno exactly what happened, but a rock spire shot out and it looked like it was coming for me, but then it turned and impaled her," Clay said. Albert looked down, thinking to himself for a moment before nodding.

"Strange thing. Do you know why they killed her?" Albert asked.

"Why they killed her?" Clay said, tilting his head a bit.

"Yeah, who else would it have been but the Red Hand member that was firing those rock spires? Maybe it was some sort of personal vendetta or something," Albert said, fully knowing what he had done but trying his best to hide it from Clay.

"Oh… yeah, I'm not sure," Clay said, looking down a moment and thinking.

"So, what happened to you, anyways? You were passed out when I came to the group, Vincent was still carrying soldiers over to the Humvees while Adam and Julie were making sure Vale was secured. Nobody saw what happened," Clay said. Albert hesitated, quickly thinking of a story.

"I got attacked by one of the Red Hand members. I don't remember much, just…" he trailed off, trying to think.

"I remember claws, some sort of hairy beast of a man," Albert said, thinking back to him and his parents facing off against Vale and Lupos in the grocery store. It had only been about a year ago, but the memories already felt like an eternity ago.

"Ah, must've been Lupos. Though, I'm surprised, you don't have any marks from his claws," Clay said, his brow furrowing as he looked over Albert's face and arms.

Albert dropped his head down, tightly closing his eyes behind a wall of hair.

"I got lucky, I guess… but after he saw that Red Hand girl get stabbed, he retreated," Albert lied.

"Weird. But that must mean they were after us, specifically, right? If they were willing to target us instead of grabbing Vin, they must have had some reason to go after us." Clay suggested.

Albert thought for a minute, hoping his lie didn't somehow snowball out of control.

"Definitely could be. But I'm still wondering what made them retreat in the first place?" Albert said, bringing a hand up to his chin in thought.

"I'm not sure. Maybe it was because we outsmarted them? They seemed to rely on their abilities to fight and simply tried to divide and conquer us, while we had a plan that negated each of them, one by one. Maybe they realized they couldn't win in a straight battle?" Clay concluded, as Adam and Bullpup walked up to them.

"If anyone asks you two, we never captured Vin Vale. Tell them he got away with the rest of the Red Hand who ambushed us," Adam said, seeing both of them nod before he and Bullpup approached the MSF officers, a total of 8 of them getting out of 4 vehicles, along with a Humvee donning a large red cross on the sides and top.

It was hours before the road was cleared of the rock spires, and the soldiers and Titan Squad all debriefed and sent back to base, where Adam requested for a return to their Headquarters, which was all too quickly accepted by the Chancellor. Titan squad was transported back to their HQ, where Adam asked that only he and Julie watch Vale until further notice. Clay, Albert and Vincent were effectively locked out of the lab for the duration of Vale's stay, and once everyone was settled back in, Julie and Adam headed down to the lab to confront and interrogate Vale.

It was dark in the lab, and while Adam stared through the clear walls at the Red Hand's leader, who sat motionless and silent in the back of the small room, Julie walked to her fridge to get him some food. She opened the freezer section, staring at the inside of it…

The freezer was still half full of Salisbury steak dinners.

Julie stared blankly for a moment before sighing, taking one out and preparing it for Vale.

"Where is your home?" Adam asked. Vale stared at the floor, shaking slightly.

"Where are all these Wild Ones coming from?" Adam further pressed. Again, Vale gave no reply.

"How many Magic Users are left? How are so many still in Tarren?" Adam continued, his voice growing increasingly frustrated. He crossed his arms and leaned back against the cell behind him, sighing. Julie brought the plastic tray over and opened the small slot on the glass wall near the floor, sliding the tray along with a fork along the floor through it and into his cell. Vale looked at the food for a moment, before looking back down in front of him.

After a minute of thinking, Adam asked,

"Do you know what happens to Magic Users when they're sent to the Capital?"

Vale's eyes darted to him, the young man nearly holding his breath at the mention of it.

"So you do… at least, you know what we do- that no Magic-User that has been sent there ever leaves. So, you know that they are most likely all executed," Adam said, approaching the glass wall and crossing his arms again.

"As long as we see use in your staying here, we won't send you to the Capital. They don't know you're here, so unless we deem you a lost cause and tell them we captured you, you'll stay here, where we'll feed you and house you. All we ask is your cooperation," Adam told him.

Vale looked up at him for a moment, before looking down at his hand, a small flame sparking from his palm, about the size of a match light.

"These dampeners your country came up with are much more advanced than anything Clemence ever used…" Vale remarked.

"Clemence… what makes you bring them up?" Adam asked.

"Most of the Red Hand are stuck in the old ways of Clemence. Thinking that if they mimic the way Clemence took over the amount of land they did, then Magic Users could have a place in this new world," Vale admitted.

"You sound like you and the Red Hand aren't a part of this world. What are you hiding from us?" Adam asked, his brow furrowing as he leaned on the glass with one hand.

Vale stopped, looking down, thinking for a moment.

"Your squad has come in contact with Exitium and his lackey, haven't they?" He asked.

"The armor-clad telekinetic and the cryokinetic. We have," Adam replied.

"Well, the fact that those two aren't here to kill me now means that I'm not telling you a thing. They're the ones tasked with making sure you Tarrenians don't find out the truth," he replied.

Adam looked over the boy for a moment, his eyes narrowing.

"Your outfit… besides the lack of a helmet, you're dressed like a soldier from Clemence back in the second Great War. Why is that?" Adam asked.

Vale paused for a moment, looking over himself before looking back to Adam.

"I already told you. The Red Hand believes that recreating Clemence is what's needed, here on the surface. To do that, they want to create their looks just like everything else," he said.

Adam stared at Vale a moment before backing off.

"Well, if you don't want to tell us any more than that, we'll just contact the Capital," Adam said. Julie looked to him, her eyes widening. Adam walked away, Julie staying behind as Vale lowered his head again, his eyes widening in realization.

It was hours before Vale would speak again.

Julie sighed, bringing her computer chair over and sitting down. She kept watch over Vale for about an hour in silence, taking time to care for the others in their cells, replacing sedative and nutrient IV bags. Vale looked over the other cells for a second, then focused his gaze on Julie.

"So, what are you doing here? Experimenting on people?" he asked. Julie paused, her head snapping to face him.

"Experimenting? No!" she replied, walking out of a cell and approaching his own, crossing her arms. Vale slowly stood, looking over them.

"Then, what are you doing?" he queried, raising an eyebrow.

"Well, mainly just trying to find their anchors. These are all Double Users," Julie said, " I'm trying to stabilize them and get them to a state where I can talk with them,"

Vale looked down, processing her reply.

"Double Users? I thought Tarrenians called them 'Wild Ones' or something like that," He said.

"Well, most do, but I and most of Titan Squad are trying to advocate for Magic Users, so I feel like 'Double User' is a better term for the offspring of two Magic Users,"

Vale looked down for a moment, chuckling a bit to himself as he considered the term.

"Well, I have to say, I'm surprised. Most of us thought that Tarrenians held nothing but hatred for Magic Users after the Great Wars," Vale admitted.

"Well, most of the civilians do, no thanks to our leader, but I, for one, understand that they are still people. Double Users, Singulars like you and me, Beastials, and even the first-generation Magic Users- none of them were monsters, just people following orders back then, and now people just trying to live," Julie explained as she stepped back, leaning on the other cell again. Vale slowly stepped forward to the middle of his cell.

"I can understand, but you do know the risk that comes with that philosophy, right? If any of these guys get free, they'll most likely be pretty angry," Vale said.

"Yeah, I understand. But I'd rather try to help than slaughter them like animals," Julie replied sarcastically.

"Killing isn't really your strong suit, is it? You and your commander saved my life. Do you think that was really the right decision?" he questioned. A smug grin was on his face as he spoke, crossing his arms.

"Oh, you're definitely gonna face consequences for your actions. But I'm glad I'm getting to peek into your head for a bit before that happens," Julie said, chuckling a bit, causing the smile to fade from Vale's face.

"Well, you're the first person from here I've met that doesn't want our people to die. But that being said, why are you fighting for Tarren if you know they all hate you?" he asked, walking up to the clear barrier between them.

"I was born here. I was raised in Tarren, and I never met another Magic-User before the commander," Julie shared, shrugging, "but that doesn't mean I don't know what I am. I just want to do good for other people, other Magic Users like Adam and Clay," she added, her cheeks flushing slightly.

"I suppose I can understand that... though, at least one of your squad mates doesn't share your pacifism," Vale replied, stepping back from the glass and picking up the TV dinner.

"Well, you and your wolf friend kind of killed his mother, I'd be mad about it, too," Julie expressed with a bit of malice in her words.

"Yeah, we did, but it's not like your government is any better. You don't even know who's leading your country, do you?" Vale looked back at her, his brow furrowing.

"What, you mean Chancellor Ambrose? What about him?" Julie asked, one of her eyebrows raised in confusion.

"Your commander said it earlier. I know what happens to our kind in that MSF facility, and it's not good. You at least had the sense to not send all of us that you catch, but you don't understand what you're doing for those Government bastards!" Vale snapped, setting the tray near where he was sitting before and walking back to the wall between him and Julie.

"So why don't you tell us so we can do something with the information? If it's something that we can stop, and that we should stop, we can try," Julie urged, resting a forearm on the glass and leaning against it as she spoke.

"I don't know specifics, but I do know about the ceremony. We found a former member who escaped the facility. She didn't tell us everything, but she lost her powers and was dying, something in her blood was drained, I think," Vale said, putting a hand on the wall. His expression was stricken with grief, remembering the tragedy.

"They removed the mana from her blood...? But how?" Julie asked.

"Meta magic. A special few of the 100,000 soldiers that were given the mana injections had abilities that only affected other magic abilities, like your new friends. Speaking of which," Vale said, crossing his arms and standing straight again, "considering you two have seen Exitium, I'm sure you know what he and his little crony are after, right?" He asked.

Julie was nodding along as she listened to him speak. "Well... to be honest, we have no idea. We've seen them twice, once they killed one of my patients here, the other time... they were after Clay and Albert, before we knew or even they knew that they were Magic Users..." Julie admitted, trailing off as she dove into her thoughts.

"Bingo. They've wanted to get their hands on your anti-magic pals for years now," Vale said.

"So, are you gonna tell me what's so special about them?" Julie asked, shrugging.

"I'm surprised you haven't figured that out yourselves already," Vale told her.

❖◆❖◆❖◆❖

Albert and Vincent were in the command room, sitting and talking when Albert froze, with a sense of extreme deja vu, like he had seen this exact scene before. Instantly, he stood.

"Something's about to happen," he said. Between the time at Basic Training and the deja vu he had just before Exitium killed Carter, Albert had figured out a pattern, and now just had to figure out what it meant. That was when a group of black SUV's rolled into the HQ's underground parking area. Seeing them on the security feed, Albert and Vincent immediately went down the elevator to see what was going on. As they approached, a squad of MSF soldiers, all dressed similar to the normal military, donning black tactical pants, combat boots, and body armor vests, but with helmets and bandanas rather than ballistic masks, all approached, rifles drawn as they yelled at the two Titan Squad members to stand down. Once they both surrendered, they were put into cuffs and sat beside one of the SUV's.

"The hell is going on here? Why are we being detained?!" Vincent asked, anger evident in his voice.

"Shut your mouth, damn hellspawns!" one of the soldiers barked. Two stayed to guard the two men as the rest moved up the stairs.

❖◆❖◆❖◆❖

"Tell me, did you see that rock spire that killed one of our own?" Vale asked, raising his chin a bit. Julie thought back, nodding.

"Yeah, I saw. We all figured it was some personal vendetta between two of your members," Julie replied.

"Heh, no, almost all of us are like family to each other. Look, back in Clemence, there was a-" Vale was suddenly interrupted by a crash from the door to the lab opening.

The sound of a gun stock hitting flesh sent Clay down the stairs and to the metal catwalk at the end of the room; one MSF soldier training his weapon at Clay and another retaining him while the others, 6 in total, moved down the stairs, weapons trained on Julie and on the cell that held Vale.

As everyone was pulled out into the parking lot, there was outrage among everyone but Adam, who looked as steadfast as ever. He seemed to know what was going on more than anyone else, though he said nothing as they sat him down with everyone else, all of them cuffed and dampeners set on them.

However, as the soldiers went to put dampeners on Clay and Albert…
POP! POP!

The red lights on the dampeners shattered, each with a loud pop, throwing bits of tiny glass on the ground.

"Are these things faulty?" one of the soldiers asked another, who shrugged. Their commander stepped out from the back seat of one of the SUV's, looking over the men. A group of trucks entered the parking garage behind them. From these trucks, a group of people in medical scrubs got out with stretchers and moved towards the elevator.

"How long were you all planning to keep these things under cover?" the commander asked, while two of the medical outfitted personnel approached Vale. Despite his struggling, they strapped his arms and legs together with cloth straps, set him on a stretcher, and brought him into one of the trucks, planning to be followed by the Double Users that Julie held in her cells, and the ones underground last. The stretchers were fairly wider than the average person, with tracks on the sides that perfectly fit the wheels on the bottom to allow them to stack on top of one another.

"I want to speak to the Chancellor," Adam said blankly, the rest of the squad staying silent and letting him speak for them.

"Oh, I assure you, the Chancellor wants a word with you, too. You've all been summoned to Rotun to speak with him yourselves. Keeping dozens of Wild Ones hidden away, harboring the leader of a known terrorist organization… this paints a very bad picture," the commander commented.

"And how did you come upon this information?" Vander Esch asked.

"I didn't, personally. That's a question for Chancellor Ambrose. We're gonna leave out with you five while the rest of the MSF personnel take care of your wild buddies here and take them to the MSF facility. I think by the time he decides what to do with all of you, they should be arriving in town. Very well, you could die at the same time as them. How poetic would that be?" The commander chuckled and made a gesture to wrap things up. The soldiers threw all 5 Titan squad members into their SUV's and left the HQ for Rotun while a total of 7 trucks filled the garage.

The squad was silent throughout the 2-hour trip, Vander Esch keeping his composure while the rest wore a similar grim expression to Vale when he was in the cell; wide eyes, a blank stare at the floor, their heads rushing with too many thoughts at once.

As the SUV's approached the Capitol building of Tarren, Julie finally spoke up, who was sitting beside Adam, while Clay and Vincent sat in another car, and Albert sat alone in the back vehicle of the small convoy.

"Adam, what are we gonna do now?" Julie whispered to him.

"Survive," he stated, his brow furrowing as he kept his gaze forward.

The squad was brought into the Capital and sat in a conference room, still handcuffed but now at least able to talk freely while they were alone.

"There was a reason I told you not to keep those Wild Ones around! Even if you had a breakthrough with them, look where disobeying our orders like that got us!" Vincent blurted out angrily at Julie.

"Yeah, it got us in a prime position to capture the leader of the Red Hand! What did you propose we do to track him down? Invent some technology that isn't anywhere near possible for these times!" Julie responded with just as much intensity.

"Hey! The Mana detector was a great idea, if we could have gotten some funding and an engineer or two to design it!" Vincent responded; Clay and Albert just sat and listened to the bickering while Adam sat with his eyes closed, his expression still determined as he fell into a deep thought.

"In any case, we never even found out what was at those geysers, so we don't know how much Carter gave us!" Julie said, her face turning red. Vincent stared at her before sighing, leaning back in his seat.

"So, what's the plan?" Clay asked, looking at Adam.

"I don't have one," he stated, to the surprise of everyone else in the room.

"We aren't here because of what we are, or because we failed. We don't know what's going to happen next, and from what I hear, the topic of why we're here is debatable on whether it was right or wrong. So, without your full support and trust, I can't make a plan. For all we know, Vincent will be offered a place in their ranks while myself and Julie are executed for harboring both Wild Ones and Vale. My plan, currently, is to let the Chancellor show his hand, and react accordingly," Vander Esch told them.

To that point, most of everyone agreed, and the room went silent for about a minute before Chancellor Ambrose walked in.

"My apologies for the delay," he said, taking a seat at the head of the table.

"Now, I have to say. I'm extremely disappointed in all of you. Everything you've done for Tarren, between the combat against Wild Ones, the fighting against that awful Red Hand organization, and your strengths as soldiers, I can't believe you all have put me in such a position," Chancellor Ambrose continued a passive- aggressive lecture for about 10 minutes about their actions, who all had a serious part in it, and a bit of sidetracking, before he got to the end.

"I feel like this Nation needs Titan Squad, considering the Red Hand and the Wild Ones are still causing issues. But I think there needs to be a change in leadership. Sergeant Vander Esch is too lenient on things outside of the main directive, which is what I believe caused this issue. So, here's the situation. If I court-martial you all, most likely the argument will be made that you're helping and harboring the Red Hand. I know that's false, but between hiding their leader, and holding these Wild Ones, which we all know are used by the Red Hand as a distraction for soldiers while they enact their plans, it could be a well-made argument. We need to establish some harsher ground rules and punishments for breaking these rules,"

"If you want to remove my authority over Titan Squad, I understand. I'll do my best to fight as a foot soldier rather than a commander," Adam said blankly. Chancellor Ambrose looked over the squad for a moment, before sighing.

"No. I'm going to be honest," Ambrose began as he stood, walking around the table behind everyone, his eyes scanning over them.

"My biggest problem isn't your attempt to find the truth behind these Wild Ones and the Red Hand's emergence. It's that you disobeyed my orders and your directive. And more than anything, that you didn't communicate your intent to begin with," Ambrose said, putting a hand on Clay's shoulder.

Instantly, Clay felt a surge of electricity throughout his body. Every nerve in his body was overloaded with information, as if it felt every feeling imaginable at the same time.

As he kept walking, just as fast as the feeling appeared, it vanished, and Clay was left staring at the Chancellor as he continued.

"Sergeant Johnson, Privates Barrett and Barrett, the three of you are dismissed. You'll all be sat down outside and wait for the clean-up to finish at your HQ, then you'll be taken back there and are to wait for your next assignment. Sergeants Alvarez and Vander Esch, I want to speak to you two in private," The Chancellor said. Clay was speechless as he, Albert and Vincent stepped outside.

"Now, I'm going to ask you a few questions. Your fates will be decided by your answers. And, this is all off-record, so I expect the truth from you two," Chancellor Ambrose began, "Now. Who was it who came up with the idea to hold Wild Ones within your HQ?" Ambrose asked.

"Mine, sir," Julie blankly stated, staring at the table in front of her as Adam kept his posture and expression straight.

"Alright. When did you build this lab within the HQ that I never saw?" Ambrose asked.

"When the structure was built, Sergeant Alvarez asked for an off-the-books area to conduct her research. I added a floor to the building plans that included no access to the elevator to hide it from officials," Adam told him. Ambrose nodded a bit, before continuing to his next question.

"Were there any successful cases? Any of the Wild Ones say anything meaningful?" Ambrose asked, leaning back on the wall.

"Yes, sir. Thanks to Clay's ability, we were able to have a conversation with one of them. He said his name was Carter, and while we're not sure what to make of most of what he said, he did tell us that he woke up near the geyser fields one day, and roamed the land for food before he was chased by Brakata's soldiers into our territory, which was when we captured him," Julie said.

"So, that's why you wanted to explore the geyser fields... alright. Where is this 'Carter' now?" Ambrose asked. Julie froze for a second before Adam spoke up.

"He was killed by Exitium and Lance, the same pair who attacked Albert and Clay a few weeks ago. They appeared from nowhere in the lab and killed Carter. They used some sort of transportation magic, so we believe they may be part of a Magic-User organization we have not encountered until now," Adam shared.

"So, the Red Hand aren't our only enemies… good to know. So, what about Vale? Why did you keep his presence from the MSF when they asked for your report?" Ambrose replied.

"We believed they would take him before we got a chance to find out more about where the Red Hand is coming from. The only thing we were able to find out is that the purpose of the men who killed Carter is to prevent us from learning the truth. Their job is to protect their organization's secrets," Adam said.

Ambrose nodded, rubbing his chin a bit.

"So, you two want to find out where these Wild Ones, and the Red Hand, are coming from," Ambrose concluded, staring at the table for a minute.

"Tell me, have you been filling out reports about the Wild Ones you've been sending to the Capital?" he asked, causing a pause from both the Sergeants.

"Yes, sir," Adam blankly said.

"Do you know how many different Wild One powers you've observed from captured ones?" He questioned further.

"From what I remember, a hundred and thirty-six," Adam replied.

"So, in one year, you've captured sixty-eight Wild Ones that you brought to the Capital. Tell me, how many were in your HQ?" Ambrose asked. Another second of silence followed.

"Forty-five," Julie said quietly.

"So, you've kept almost as many in your pockets as you've brought to the MSF facility, correct?" Ambrose asked.

"Sir, with all due respect, these are people we are talking about," Julie said, looking up to him. Ambrose chuckled, standing straight and crossing his arms, looking at her.

"They're people? Sergeant, people don't willingly blow themselves to smithereens just to get revenge on others. They don't wildly attack anything in their path! They don't rely on some facet of their lives to keep their sanity!" Ambrose said, raising his voice.

"These are not human beings we're speaking about. They're wild animals that I tasked you with capturing and bringing to the MSF for disposal," He said.

Disposal, Julie thought…

"Sir, if I may ask, what happens to the Double Users we send to the MSF facility?" Julie questioned. Ambrose paused, looking down and wiping his mouth and chin.

"I am afraid that's classified information. I don't think you want to know, anyways," he replied.

"I think I've made my decision. The other three will continue their work for Titan Squad, but will be reassigned to a different commander. You two…" Ambrose thought for a moment.

"I don't think we need your services any longer. Julie, Adam, I'm sorry… but you've both become a liability. If the public found out about this incident, they would riot. If the Red Hand were to attack and release them, it would have been even worse chaos. You two are to be sent to the MSF facility immediately," Ambrose said.

* * *

Vincent and Albert sat silently as the three men outside awaited their commander and Julie to return, but they never did.

"Alright, load up," one of the two soldiers who were guarding them said, walking towards the SUV's.

"Hey, wait a minute! Where's J-… Sergeant Alvarez? Or Sergeant Vander Esch?!" Clay yelled out. Albert and Vincent both looked over at the soldiers, their brows furrowing.

"I'm just following my orders. Now get in; we're headed back to your HQ," the commander said.

"Hey, hold on, we're not leaving without our commander; he gives us orders, not you," Albert protested. Vincent kept silent, but stayed beside Albert, gently grabbing his arm.

POP!

"The hell you're not, get moving!" One of the soldiers yelled at him, walking over with his rifle.

"Why don't you make me?" Albert confronted, and under his breath, he whispered, "Dagger,"

In his hand, a small blade manifested, and he used it to cut against the handcuffs, prying one of the chains until it broke. Vincent did the same just as one of the men lunged at him with the stock of his gun.

Vincent sidestepped the blow, swinging and hitting the soldier in the nose, knocking him to the ground. Albert made sure his dagger dissipated before it crossed Clay's sight before he jumped forward, grabbing the other man's gun just as he had raised it. Two bullets fired into the ground before Albert head-butted the man in the nose, taking the weapon and hitting the soldier in the sternum with the rifle.

Clay's eyes widened as Vincent walked over, using his dagger to pry the chain off on Clay's cuffs too.

"What's the plan?" Clay asked.

"Well, if they're not gonna bring the Commander and Julie back to us, we're taking them back," Vincent said, "I don't agree with Julie on how to deal with Magic Users, but they're our friends and our brother and sister-in-arms. If they're not coming with us, we're not going anywhere,"

"Yeah, let's go get them. I doubt Clay could stand himself if something happened to Julie," Albert said, dropping the rifle.

The three walked back inside, Vincent pushing a single guard aside and into a table as they pushed open the doors to the conference room, seeing it empty.

"What? It's only been like five minutes. Where did they go?" Clay asked. A bit of panic was evident in his voice. Vincent looked to the guard, picking him up and pinning him to the wall.

"Sergeants Alvarez and Vander Esch. Where are they?" Vincent interrogated, his face shadowed from the lights in the middle of the room and his eyes wide and filled with rage. The guard, in a suit rather than a military uniform, struggled against his grip.

"He said you were getting reassigned, that they're being… decommissioned," the guard admitted as he tried to push Vincent's arm off him, to no avail.

"I didn't ask what happened, I asked where they were taken," Vincent said. Clay and Albert watched on, both of them silent and diverting eye contact with the guard.

"Th-they're headed to the MSF facility, across town. Why… I thought you hellspawn didn't have friends," The guard said, defiant even in the position he was in. Vincent shook his head and pushed him to the side, walking towards the door.

"Come on, let's go. I know where the facility is… Worst case scenario? We have to break in to get them out," Vincent said. Clay followed; Albert hesitated as he walked a bit behind them.

"You guys realize if we try and pull some kind of rescue operation, the government will hunt us down? We'll be fugitives?" Albert warned. Vincent stopped, turning around and staring into Albert's eyes.

"Do you realize what I do in Titan Squad, Albert? I fight. I keep innocent people from getting hurt, whether it's by the Red Hand, or by Wild Ones. I don't need Government permission to do that. And the way I see it, Julie and Adam are innocent. I'm protecting them, too, just from the MSF instead of actual Magic Users. I need them alive, Albert," Vincent said. Albert was taken aback for a moment.

"I wasn't protesting, by any means, just making sure you guys knew what this would cause. I'm with you, absolutely," Albert affirmed, raising his hands in surrender.

"Alright, then let's go get them," Clay replied, and off the three of them went, towards the MSF facility, about 2 miles away.

Chapter 6

❖ ✦ ❖ ✦ ❖ ✦ ❖

I t was about 10 minutes of running down the sidewalks before the three of them saw the set of trucks that had been at their HQ hours before, 6 of them in a line stopped in the middle of a crowd of unmoving cars that kept growing by the minute.

"Why are they stopped?" Clay asked, but as they approached, they spotted spires that shot up from the road into the wheels of the trucks.

"Dammit, the Red Hand is here! They probably came for Vale!" Albert said, his fists balling up with anger.

"Hey, stay focused. If we're fugitives from Tarren, we don't need to fight or capture them. Protect civilians if you need to, but we're here for Julie and Adam, nobody else!" Vincent called as a small explosion echoed through the streets. Down the road, one of the trucks' back doors had been blown open, and a pair of figures entered the truck, slipping into the shadow within.

"Alright, so how do you propose we do this? Think they might be in one of the trucks with the others?" Albert asked.

❖ ✦ ❖ ✦ ❖ ✦ ❖

Adam and Julie sat in the back of an armored truck, rolling down the road. Julie and Adam were without guards in the back, though the soldiers in the cab were listening in.

"I'm sorry for getting you into this, dragging you down with me…." Julie said, her head hanging low as Adam continued to sit straight.

"My decisions were my own, Julie. Ever since we met in that prison and Ambrose proposed the idea of Titan Squad, I've supported you and your curiosities about what we are," He said. Julie nodded a bit, sighing.

"I know, but even so, I feel like this is all my fault. Now we're being sent to our death, essentially," Julie said, looking at him with tears in her eyes, "How can you stay so calm?" She asked.

"Hey, don't you two get any funny ideas!" One of the soldiers yelled at them, punching the metal door that separated the cab from the back, where they sat.

"For two reasons," Adam replied to Julie's question.

"One, I think everyone on the squad knows you and Clay have feelings for one another. There's no doubt in my mind he'll be coming to help you," Adam said, pausing as another strike against the metal turned their attention to the cab.

"The hell did I just say?! Keep talking like that and I'll make sure all they find when they reach us are corpses!" The soldier up front yelled. The truck stopped. Adam looked into the eyes of the soldier. Then, he looked back at Julie.

"Two, either of us could stand up and remove the other's dampener. And I believe we could beat the soldiers up front even without our abilities," Vander Esch said.

"Oh, think so?" The soldier said, opening the door and walking into the back, slamming the door behind him.

"Damn traffic, the hell's going on up there?" The driver asked.

The soldier walked over and bent down, his face level with Adam's as Julie stayed silent, watching.

"How about I take those cuffs off you and beat your ass so bad you'll put them back on yourself?" He said, hands on his knees as he spoke in Adam's face.

"No weapons, no magic abilities. I'm up for a fight," Adam said, finally breaking his composure, seeing the soldier's rage in his eyes.

"Oh I bet you are," The soldier said, before slapping Vander Esch across the face, knocking him a bit to the side.

"You think I'm stupid?! You damn demons never fight a fair fight, we've known that for a hundred years now!" The soldier said, sending a strike into Adam's gut. Julie's eyes widened and she brought a leg up, sending her boot into the soldier's tailbone and knocking him forward, pushing his head into the side of the truck's bed. The soldier fell to the floor as Julie stood, kicking him in the chest.

"Hey!" The driver looked back and yelled, unbuckling his seatbelt.

But before he could get out of his seat, the sound of crushed and warped metal echoed through the truck; A rock spire ripped through the front of the truck, stabbing into the chest of the soldier and pinning him to the seat, the edge of the now blood-covered spike pushing all the way until the tip of it poked through the metal that separated the cab and the bed.

Julie froze, seeing the rock spire, Adam sitting up and looking at it himself. The two looked at one another as heavy footsteps approached the back of the truck. They both stood away from the doors, unsure of what was happening.

The doors were pulled, groaning in protest before the lock that held them together slipped off the other door. They both swung open, a pair of Magic Users standing on the ground in front of Julie and Adam.

The first was Ruby, the same one who Tarren almost captured before Lupos saved her, and the second was an unfamiliar one. His skin was Grey and leathery, and he had a horn sticking from his forehead, like a rhinoceros. He stood at a hefty 6'8" and at least 400lbs of muscle, with the physique of a strongman.

"Not here, either. Who are you two?" The man asked.

"Hey, wait a minute, I know you guys," Ruby said, hopping up to the back of the truck, her brow furrowing as she crossed her arms, "Did Tarren decide they were through with you?" She asked. Julie paused, looking at Adam, who brought back his composure before speaking to the two.

"We were sent to the MSF facility for hiding your leader from the government. Had we not, he most likely would already be dead. I'd ask that you return the favor and let us leave. We pose no harm and have no reason to fight you," Adam said. Ruby laughed at his words, shaking her head.

"How about instead, we take you two with us and let him decide your fates after we get him out of here?" Ruby said, grabbing Adam by the arm and pushing him towards the Rhino-like user, who promptly grabbed him. Julie met the same circumstance a second before the two of them walked towards the next truck. Ruby made two spires out of the concrete on the sidewalk, and Adam and Julie were hooked on them, standing with the spires behind them between their backs and their cuffed wrists.

Clay, Albert, and Vincent made their way down the road, and the first truck they saw opened up from the back. A couple of the Wild Ones on stretchers had been rolled out of the truck and were restrained in the middle of the street, and a rustling came from inside the truck. Albert paused while the other two kept moving, slowly peeking into the back and seeing a figure turn and start to walk out, both of them freezing when they recognized the other.

Clay and Vincent looked back at Albert as he stared into the truck, before he went for his gun.

"Albert, wait!" Clay yelled, both of them running over before Lupos kept out of the truck, knocking Albert to the ground with a shoulder tackle into his chest, the clothing on him preventing Lupos from changing.

Vincent summoned a pair of throwing knives, planting a foot and raising one in preparation as Clay jumped between Lupos and Albert.

"Stop! We're not here to fight you!" Clay yelled, Lupos stopping as Albert's gun slid to the curb of the sidewalk.

"Why else would you be here? You knew we wouldn't let Vale get MSF'ed, so come on! Let's end this here and now!" Lupos yelled, staying in place but raising his claws in a fighting stance.

"Tarren betrayed us! We came to rescue the others in our squad and ran away from the MSF with them. We aren't your enemies, not now," Clay said.

"Bullshit, we're not," Albert said as he stood again, eyeing Lupos.

"This is the bastard that killed our mother. You know I want both him and Vale dead," Albert said. Clay turned to him.

"Albert! If we sit here and fight, we'll just wear ourselves out so the military can finish us! We need to find Julie and Adam and get out of here!" Clay said to him, Lupos slowly easing his stance.

"That's our plan for Vale. Pick him up and get out," Lupos said, looking to Vincent a second, who kept his knives ready. Clay looked at him for a second, gesturing for him to lower his knife.

"Look, I know we don't like you guys and you don't like us. But now isn't the time or place to fight. How about this, if we find Vin or you guys find Julie and Adam, we'll let him go with you and them with us. Fair?" Clay said, Albert and Vincent both angry but lowering their stances, Albert walking and picking up his gun, stowing it in its holster again.

"Alright… deal. How will we contact each other?" Lupos asked, before Clay tossed him his radio.

"We'll turn to frequency 6. That's our squad's private channel. Use it and let us know where you guys are after you leave if we need to switch. I'll take the radio back when we do, if that's the case," Clay said.

"And if we don't end up needing to meet?" Lupos asked.

"Then keep it. I don't think I'll need it anyways," Clay said, looking back to Albert and Vincent as the three of them moved to the next truck, Lupos moving to the next one past theirs.

As Ruby and the Rhino-man searched the next truck, the fourth one opened out of 8, the sound of military humvees rumbling in the distance, approaching fast.

"Hey Ruby, slow them down!" The Rhino-man said.

Ruby nodded, walking to the edge of the intersection and crouching down, touching her hands to the road. She took a deep breath, feeling the humvees approaching through the earth.

Raising her hands, Ruby yelled, and a row of the spires shot up from the ground, rising above the humvees and blocking their path towards the trucks. She then put her hands together, two more rows rising from the side streets near the humvees, stabbing through a couple of the vehicles and blocking the rest from using those roads to go around the original blockade.

Ruby looked back, calling out as the Rhino-man searched the truck for Vin Vale.

"Wyndham, hurry! These roadblocks won't hold them for--" Ruby said, interrupted by a gunshot firing into the road beside the girl, followed by a flurry of gunfire as she ran into the truck for cover.

The Rhino-man, Wyndham, looked back as he confirmed the last stretcher in the truck wasn't Vale.

"They're in the buildings. I couldn't see where the fire was coming from," Ruby said, panting and looking back towards the buildings before a bullet sank into the metal of the truck just beside her head, forcing her to pull back into the truck.

"Dammit. Can't get a good visual to retaliate," She said, thinking as she looked to Wyndham, who stood looking out to try and see a way out.

"Hey, I have an idea," Ruby said.

"That's a lot of gunfire...." Clay said as the three approached the truck. Vincent summoned a long crowbar, and the three of them all pushed to force the door open.

Inside, they searched through the nine stretchers, noticing a black spire that jutted through the front of the cab, and another jutting out from the original, both of them stabbing through the two soldiers in the seats. Clay sighed, shaking his head as he went back to looking for the Red Hand leader.

Vincent looked back as he saw 3 black Humvees pulling up at the back of the traffic jam, local police blocking off the streets and evacuating civilians. At the same time, MSF soldiers stepped out of the vehicles, rifles drawn as they moved toward the truck convoy. The sound of gunfire echoed from somewhere outside of town as if the areas outside of town had become a war zone.

"Soldiers incoming, hurry it up," Vincent said, creating a riot shield to ensure no pot shots entered the truck. Clay looked back outside at the evacuating civilians, thinking as he looked at Albert.

"Alright, I have a plan to allow ourselves to escape. But you're not gonna like it," He said. Albert looked over, narrowing his eyes.

Titan Squad moved out of the truck as the soldiers approached the truck they had been in, and a moment later, the 12 soldiers were bombarded by a horde of Wild Ones. All of them bearing various powers, including one that spat venom, another whose skin he superheated before grabbing the soldiers, burning their clothes and skin underneath.

Immediately, the men started firing, scaring most of the Wild Ones off and killing three of them that fought despite the gunfire. Four of their men were seriously injured, forcing the rest to pull them back out of the fray.

Clay, Albert and Vincent ran out of the truck and away while the men dragged their allies away, moving to the next truck, only two left to search.

Ruby and Wyndham were still pinned, Ruby explaining her plan before Wyndham stepped out into the streets, hands up as he looked up the buildings. One was made from mostly metal, and the other was brick.

"Right side, 6th story, first window," He said. Nothing had happened just yet, but as Wyndham watched the men who aimed weapons at him, he continued speaking, his voice low but enough for Ruby to hear.

"4th story, third window. 3rd story, second window," He said. He then looked to the other building, cursing under his breath seeing the building's design.

"Now!" He yelled, running at the building. Bullets began to fly, several slamming into his back and bouncing off before Ruby moved out of the truck. The outside walls of the brick building caved in as rock spires soared inside the building from the walls. The gunfire stopped from the right side, and Wyndham got just below the metal building, out of range for the shooters.

With Wyndham pointing up, Ruby nodded and rose several rock spires from the road, slamming them into the windows of the building. From what they saw, no more gunfire rang out from the building above Wyndham, and he approached Ruby again, chuckling.

"Nice one. Good thing I was with you, I don't think anyone else on the team could have-" Wyndham began, before Ruby saw the barrel of one rifle in the window below where she sent her spires. One gunshot fired, louder and more powerful than any of the ones they had heard so far.

A .50 caliber bullet ripped through the shoulder of Wyndham, ripping out the other side and falling onto the road as Ruby stared at the sniper, her expression quickly turning from shock to rage as she sent a spire from the brick building across the road and into the window she saw the sniper in. Blood splattered off the window as the sniper was stabbed by the spire and was pushed out of view from the road, sending shattered glass and shrapnel down onto the road nearby.

Kneeling down, Ruby helped Wyndham turn over to see the huge chunk of meat missing from his shoulder. She was panicked, unsure of what she could do to help him, when she looked over and noticed an older woman walking out of one of the trucks. Ruby paused as the woman looked towards them, making eye contact before she began walking over. Ruby stood while Wyndham struggled to keep breathing.

As the woman approached, Ruby watched her drift past the girl and approach Wyndham, kneeling down beside him. Ruby watched as the woman put her hand over his wound, a light emitting from her hand that slowly generated more skin to cover up the wound.

"A healer?" She asked, kneeling beside the woman, who only nodded.

"I may have been cast out from the Ark for having two abilities, but that doesn't mean I can't do some good for people. Just don't ask me to use my other power. I don't ever want to use it again," She said as she stopped the mending of his wound while leaving only a small hole in his shoulder.

"Wait... what's your other ability?" Ruby said, cautiously.

"That, I'd rather not say," The woman shrugged, putting her other hand out. Another light emitted from her wrist and a stream of blood flowed from the light into the hole in Wyndham's shoulder.

"And don't worry, funny enough, I'm an O negative," The woman said with a chuckle. Ruby looked to Wyndham, whose breathing was steadying.

"Thank you… but what is your anchor, then?" Wyndham asked.

"I tried to figure that out for a long time. But helping people live seemed to make me happy, so I suppose using my abilities is what I fixated on," She said with a smile.

Ruby left Wyndham with the healing Double User and joined Lupos, seeing Titan squad and immediately getting into a fighting stance before Lupos calmed her down. They were down to the last two trucks, and he informed her of his agreement.

"What?! You realize they tried to get into… y'know… right?" She whispered to Lupos, who nodded.

"I know… but for now, they're the enemy of my enemy until we get Vin back," Lupos replied.

The groups split up, Lupos and Ruby moving to one truck and opening it, the soldiers already killed as the Red Hand began their search.

Clay, Albert and Vincent took the other truck, opening the truck with the same crowbar that Vincent made last time. Inside the truck, they heard a struggle from the bottom of the stretchers, and began unloading the stretchers to make their way to the source. It was just a minute before Lupos ran over to them.

"He's not in this one. Ruby found your people; where's Vin?" Lupos asked as Clay pushed one last stretcher off the tracks of another, holding Vin.

"Yeah, we found the bastard," Albert said, crossing his arms as Vincent cut his straps off, albeit somewhat reluctantly.

Vin was unconscious, Vincent pulling him off the stretcher, roughly pushing him to the floor of the truck.

"We have incoming!" Clay said, seeing a couple squads of MSF soldiers moving up the road past the rows of cars, headed towards them. Vincent looked to the cab, walking through the clearing between the stretchers and grabbing the pair of rifles that sat on the floorboard of the cab between the dead men's seats. He also grabbed a pair of handcuffs and their key from one of the corpses.

Vincent tossed one to Albert while Clay was given the handcuffs to secure Vin with. Clay cuffed the Red Hand leader and sat him up against the side of the truck, and Vincent and Albert began firing on the men who were approaching them.

Immediately, the MSF soldiers took cover behind the buildings and cars, out of sight from the two who fired on them.

Lupos and Ruby ran to the truck, Lupos speaking.

"You got Vale?" He asked.

"Yeah, we got him! Do you guys have Adam and Julie?" Clay asked as Vincent and Albert suppressed the MSF.

"Ruby has them a bit down the road, we'll go pick them up and get out of here. Where do we want to meet?" He asked.

"Can you guys get to where we fought last time?" Clay asked.

"I'm sure we can get there. You have a way out there?" Lupos asked.

"We can figure something out," Clay said.

"Alright, well, if you get into trouble, radio in. We can have Chris transport you all back. He was the one who was using the smoke before," Lupos briefly explained before moving out with Ruby.

"We'll let you know, but we'll meet you there no matter what!" Clay called out to Lupos as he and Ruby backed up. Ruby sent a rock spire across the road from one brick building across to the opposite sidewalk, slowing the soldiers down for Titan Squad as the Red Hand members got Wyndham and started making their way out of the area.

"Come on, let's move," Albert said, moving out of the truck; Vincent followed behind him and Clay carried Vale on his shoulders behind them.

They moved up the line a bit, seeing most of the intersections were cut off by Ruby's rock spires.

Up ahead, the group heard a heavy *Thud* against the rock spires. The sound of a large engine tumbled behind the spires, fading out a bit before the engine revved, the vehicle it powered slamming into the rock spires again, this time sending cracks throughout the spires.

"Come on, move inside one of these buildings!" Albert yelled right before a black APC came crashing through the rock it had been slamming into, finally breaking through and allowing MSF troops to flood in behind it.

Albert, Clay and Vincent all ran into the closest building they could find, keeping low to the ground, Clay struggling to carry Vale as they tried to move quickly.

The three moved up the stairs of the building about 6 stories up, then exited to watch the situation from above and look for a route to escape. Clay watched the road that they had just exited, while Vincent and Albert watched the sides and back windows, looking for a way out of the city.

"There's a pair of Humvee's at the end of the block to the North, near where the first truck is stopped. If we can find a way down there from here, or a secondary exit from the building, we can take one of them out of town and to the meeting point," Albert said, Vincent nodding.

"Why don't we just have their transporter bring us out?" Clay asked. Vincent and Albert both stared at him as Albert approached.

"For one, we would have to remove Vale's dampener, and I'm not taking the chance of having to fight him. Two, I don't trust any of those terrorists and war criminals; why the hell would I ask them to teleport me somewhere? For all we know we get scooped up in that smoke, thrown in a cell, beaten, and killed for fighting against them," Albert explained.

"We have their leader, I think that's a pretty good bargaining chip," Clay said.

"Yeah, not easy to bargain when we're in a cell and he teleports him to the other side of the bars!" Albert raised his voice, Clay finally sighing and flailing his arms in defeat.

"Fine, I get it. So, how are we gonna get down to a Humvee without alerting the MSF?" Clay asked, kneeling beside Vale, who was now conscious, staring silently at the floor. Albert looked to Vincent, thinking.

"Vincent, do you know for sure that your power is limited to weapons?" He asked. Vincent shook his head.

"Technically, as long as it's not complicated, I can conjure most anything I can hold. But, the bigger the object, the more it takes out of me," He explained.

"How about two spears and a rope long enough for us to zip line down?" Albert asked, Vincent giving him a wary expression.

"I dunno, it'll be rough if I do. I can do that to get us to a lower rooftop, though, and maybe a second line after that,"

Clay shook his head slowly, thinking as he watched the men look over the Wild Ones in their stretchers, a couple of them putting bullets in their heads. However, all at once the men decided to turn back and run back to their trucks.

"Guys, something is happening!" Clay said, while Albert and Vincent ran over to see what the situation was.

The soldiers all had their weapons raised. Clay, Albert, and Vincent watched as they moved, their eyes darting to a soldier falling, obviously from being dropped from a great height. He slammed into the top of a car, the other soldiers looking over and one going to check on him as the others watched the buildings above.

From atop the towering structures, two figures from either side of the road hurled themselves off, aiming their heads towards the ground before spreading their arms, a thin veil of skin connecting their sides to their hands, in the form of wings. They swooped down, dive-bombing the soldiers and slamming their shoulders into the soldiers and using them as human shields against the others.

Two more figures ran out from the side of the road, both with shiny, silver-like skin. They helped the two bird-like fighters against the soldiers, the MSF's bullets spraying the two silver figures, but while the force from them pushed the two people back, it didn't stop them.

"This is our chance. Let's go!" Albert said, patting Vincent on the shoulder as the three men started moving to the other side of the building. The gunfire in the distance hadn't let up; hundreds of pops from far away guns faintly echoed in the town.

Vincent summoned the zip line down to the first rooftop, handing out crossbars to use on the rope. The three of them made it down easily, Clay carrying Vale down with them. Vincent, without hesitation, let the first one disappear once they were across and began setting up the second one.

"Finally, I think we're out of this. Let's go," Albert said, letting Clay on first, Albert grabbing Vale and throwing him over his shoulder while Clay got ready to go down, Vincent behind him.

The three started down the zip line, but as Clay saw a pair of MSF soldiers, it was too late for him to say anything.

One of the soldiers fired into Vincent's shoulder, hitting the target and sending him off the line. The soldiers were joined by three others, the now 5 men surrounding Clay, Albert, Vin and Vincent at the bottom of the zip lines.

They immediately put Clay and Albert on the ground, stripping Albert of his 1911 and holding the four men down. One of them put a dampener on Vincent, and Albert, seeing Vale on the ground, cursed to himself, but feeling a handcuff go over his arm, he quickly looked to Clay, whose head was turned and held in the other direction by the soldiers.

Time seemed to slow. Albert could look and see every movement happening for a moment. The adrenaline rush of him knowing he had to do something now, but there was a limit to what he could do. Vincent was injured, Clay was useless in combat, but Vale…

Albert threw a hand in front of him, reaching out towards Vale. He could feel a faint heat flowing up his fingers and all the way to his shoulder. He focused on it, heightening it, drawing it from where it was being held down, and commanding it to rise… to rise…

POP!

A plume of fire burst from Vale, scorching his subduers and almost instantly burning away the cloth straps that had restrained him. Vale stood, the fire and heat filling him with energy. All three of the men who held the others looked at Vale, grabbing their rifles before a wave of flames flew from his hand, covering the men's upper half and sending them backward in a panic, all of them rolling and flailing their arms to try and put themselves out, but were unsuccessful.

Vale looked to the MSF soldiers, panting for a moment before he looked to Titan Squad. Clay had a hand up in fear, sitting up. Vincent was bleeding, wincing from the pain and now clutching his shoulder. However, Albert was slowly getting to his feet, staring down Vale with contempt in his eyes.

Vin walked towards him before, out of nowhere, his flames disappeared. His eyes widened as he realized what Albert had done.

"Your friends have our friends. As you can probably guess by now, we had you until the MSF took us down. I don't care what problems we have, and I should make you aware that I fully intend to kill you when I have the chance. But right now, we need help, and Lupos didn't try to kill us," Albert said. Vale was silent for a moment, looking at Clay and Vincent a moment before nodding.

"Alright, well, first we need to help this guy," Vale said, walking to Vincent while Albert and Clay followed behind.

"Someone tear some cloth off their uniform. I'll make a tourniquet," Vale said. Clay immediately tore off one of his sleeves for him and handed it over for Vale to wrap it over Vincent's wound.

"Alright, this should stop most of the bleeding, but we need to get him medical help as soon as we can," Vale said. Clay looked at Albert, who hesitated, gritting his teeth a moment before sighing and nodding to him.

"Lupos, we need that exit from Chris. We took Vale's dampener off so he should be good to go now, too," Clay said. Vale checked Vincent for dampeners, looking back at Clay.

"You guys are in contact now?" He asked. Clay nodded as Lupos' voice came over the radio.

"Got it. Transporting now," He said. One by one, they all had their vision blurred by smoke and were pulled back into a forest, Vale stepping backward. At the same time, Clay and Albert stumbled back, and Vincent was pulled back by the two metal-skinned women that Titan Squad saw earlier. They pulled him to a tree and sat him down, the Double User that Ruby had met walking towards Vincent to help him. The sun was nearly set now, barely touching the horizon as it continued its slow descent into dusk.

Wyndham, with bandages over his shoulder, walked Adam and Julie over to Titan Squad, however the rest of the Red Hand surrounded them, including the two flying men and Ruby. Upon a closer look, the two flying men were older, with brown hair, pointed ears and noses pointed up like bats.

Vale looked around a moment as Lupos approached, smiling.

"That was a hell of a situation. Glad to have you back, V," Lupos said, the two men grasping hands for a moment before Vale turned to Albert and Clay.

"Now, you two wanna tell me how you went from throwing me in a cell to busting me out?" Vale asked, crossing his arms. Clay explained what had happened while Albert watched around him, clearly on edge.

"Well, alright. So you're all fugitives now. Seems stupid that you were fighting your own kind all this time,"

At his words, Albert stared at Vale, walking towards him. Clay reached out to stop him but couldn't before Albert swung, his fist landing flush against Vale's jaw, knocking him backward and causing most of the Red Hand around them to prepare their powers to fight. Clay pulled back Albert as he started yelling.

"Are you kidding me?! You two killed my family! You sent Wild Ones to kill my family, and then you tried to kill us again right here not even a day ago!" He yelled as Clay finally pushed him back to the center of the clearing where they originally stood.

"I don't know about the rest of our squad, but to me, you two and the rest of you are nothing but psychotic murderers! Why the hell would I not want you dead?!" He asked in a rage. Lupos bared his teeth before Vale put a hand on his shoulder, standing straight again and holding his jaw before he spoke.

"I get it… Goldberg was a shit show. We killed a lot of people we shouldn't have. But after what happened to my mother, I-" Vale spoke before Albert interrupted him.

"What did my mother have to do with that?! She didn't do anything to you but stab your ass after you attacked us first, and she died trying to protect herself and me!" Albert kept yelling as Vale looked down, putting his hands on his hips.

"I know… she died protecting you, and Lupos killed her to protect me. But my point is that you all need our help. We can get you out of Tarren and to Brakata for asylum, or, if you just listen to our cause, we can possibly work together," Vale said, Albert interrupting again.

"Work together?! Why would I work together with-"Albert yelled back before Clay finally hit his brother, knocking him to the side for a second. Albert stared at the ground for a moment, then at Clay.

"Shut. The FUCK. Up," Clay said, an irritated expression on his face as he stared back at Albert before looking back to Vin and Lupos, Albert rubbing his jaw and going silent.

"First, tell us about this 'cause' of yours. Then we can decide as a group what we should do. But before that, we want the rest of our squad back," Clay said. Vin and Lupos looked at one another a second before Vale nodded. Julie and Adam were unrestrained and their dampeners were removed, allowing them to walk to the center of the ring with the Barrett brothers. Julie and Clay hugged as Adam rubbed his wrists, looking to the Red Hand leader.

"Clay… thank you," Adam said, putting his arm on Clay's shoulder. Vincent walked over to the group and passed the Red Hand members, bandages over his arm similar to Wyndham's.

"Ever since Titan Squad was formed, my goal was simply to comply with whatever the Chancellor, and later on Julie, wanted. I've had no drive to do anything but survive, and it seems I couldn't properly do that. But thanks to you and the others, I'm still able to. Thank you," He said with a smile, Clay with stars in his eyes for a moment before all of Titan Squad looked to Vale.

"Alright. Explain your intentions, then," Adam said, returning to his composed, serious stature, arms crossed.

"Our goal right now is to create a sanctuary within Tarren for Magic Users," Vin said, "A place where they don't have to be chased down, hunted, or persecuted. If there's anyone who would understand that cause, it'd be you," He pointed to Julie, who was deep in thought about what he said.

"Yeah, cause killing civilians and waging war on Tarren is the way to go about it," Albert said, sarcastically. Vale's eyes filled with rage at the mention of the attack again.

"Alright! You wanna know the truth about what happened in Goldberg? Let's talk about it. My mother was kidnapped by a Wild One who took her to Tarren! Your army found her being held hostage, killed the Wild One, and brought her to the Capital, and I never saw her again! They took her from me, so I started hating the powerless! I hated Tarrenians for what they took from me, so I burned the town she was found in! I burned

Goldberg to the ground because I wanted revenge! But you know what? I got nothing out of it but guilt and a stab wound! And Lupos was the one out of us who got blood on his hands, after he did nothing but go along with my rage! He may have stabbed her, but I killed your mother!" Vale yelled, tears welling up in his eyes.

"I killed those people! No matter who pulled the trigger, or which Wild One killed, it's my fault!" He continued, falling to his knees, hands balled into fists on his legs.

"I've had to live with that guilt... I've acknowledged it, I've done my best to forgive myself and prevent anything like that again, but dammit, you don't understand how hard it is! To not only lose my mother, but to take so many mothers and fathers of others the way I did...." Vin said, looking down. Albert stared at Vin, pausing before his anger welled up again.

"You want me to feel sorry for you? You want pity because you're sad that you did something wrong? You sound like a whiny little brat that got caught with his hand in a cookie jar! You murdered dozens of people, and now you want people to feel sorry for you?!" He yelled, both Julie and Clay holding Albert back.

Adam sighed, putting a hand on Albert's shoulder.

"You don't have to forgive him. Harbor as much anger for him as you want, but look at our situation. We still need his help," Adam said. Albert finally stopped pushing against the two, breathing heavily.

"I'm not looking for forgiveness... I'm just giving an explanation. That it wasn't just some decision I made, getting out of bed one day. I had my reasons, no matter how wrong they were," Vale said, standing.

"In any case, it's your choice. Stay with us, we'll bring you back to our current hideout in Tarren, but we can't risk Exitium visiting us, so we can't show you our home for the moment," Vale said.

"Does your home have something to do with the geysers?" Adam immediately asked, raising an eyebrow. Vale paused, looking at him.

"That was what you all were headed to look into, wasn't it?" Vale asked in response, crossing his own arms.

"We got a tip that there was something there. Checking maps, there was nothing out there. Do you have some sort of secret hiding spot that you raise Wild Ones in?" Adam asked, raising his chin a bit.

"Heh… you're way off track, but I like the investigation. Your search for knowledge is never-ending, is it?" Vin asked.

"Alright, come on, we need to go soon," Lupos said.

"Okay, okay. So, what's it gonna be?" Vin asked the squad.

After discussing for a moment, Titan Squad refused the Red Hand's offer to join their cause, and plans were made to sneak Titan Squad across the border into Brakata, where the Red Hand said there was a small sanctuary for them.

Chapter 7

◆◆◆◆◆

"I won't disagree with that. This city could use more freedom. In a way, these people are simply waiting around to die. Without any hope for their children growing up, without ambition, something has to be done,"

"ou want to know where they're actually coming from?"

"You know?"

"Yeah, I can show you. But you have to promise me something first,"

"What?"

Titan Squad and the Red Hand had camped out in the forest before getting up to leave the next morning. However, as they woke up, two people were missing from the group.

"Albert! Vincent!" Clay yelled into the forest as the whole of the group searched the forest and surrounding mountains for any sign of Vincent and Albert.

Vale and Lupos looked to the West, towards the geyser fields, the remaining Titan Squad members looked to the North, up one mountain, while half of the Red Hand members looked South up the other mountain, and the rest looked East, towards the major roadways and the military installation about 10 miles away. They all kept in radio contact as they searched, nobody coming up with any clues on the radios.

"Do you think he really did it?" Vale asked Lupos as they walked towards the geysers, steam and other gasses expelling from the holes in the earth below them.

"I dunno... but out of everyone in that squad, he's the last one I would want to see in the Ark. Noah always said that he foresaw someone destroying it, but he didn't have enough time to stop him. Even with Exitium in hand," Lupos replied, crossing his arms as they looked over the geyser field.

+ + + + + +

Clay sighed, putting his hands on his head as Julie and Adam climbed the mountain in front of him. Clay looked back over the trees, the geysers in the distance, and the valley leading out of view on Clay's left.

"What if Exitium got them? But they would've just killed us if that was the case… maybe they were looking for something and the MSF found them? But then the rest of us would've been found, too… I just don't know…." Clay said, looking down. Adam looked back at Clay for a moment, then to Julie, who was looking past the side of the mountain to the NorthWest.

"Julie… did you ever read Vincent's file when he joined Titan Squad?" He asked. Julie spun around, raising an eyebrow.

"Hmm? Of course. Why?" She asked. Adam put one foot on a rock, leaning his elbow on his knee and thinking.

"One of the big reasons I didn't trust him at first was his lack of information. It said he was born in Brakata but moved to Tarren as a child. He never specified parents, guardians, or anything else. It's like he came from thin air on Tarren's doorstep," Adam said, rubbing his chin.

"Vale and the Red Hand didn't recognize him, and when we saw Exitium in our facility, he used his throwing knives at him rather than pulling out the pistol on his hip, even though we didn't realize at the time that Exitium could do what he did. We knew he could stop bullets, but how did he know he couldn't stop his knives? Do you think he may have known more about Exitium than we did?" Adam looked to Julie, whose eyes widened in realization.

"You think Vincent could be from the same place those two came from?" She asked. Adam nodded, Clay listening in and staring at the ground for a moment.

"Do you think... he could have kidnapped Albert? Brought him back to wherever he came from?" Clay asked. Julie and Adam both looked down a minute.

"Exitium wanted you two for a reason, presumably your powers, if what Vale told us was true. You and your brother have a special kind of ability that affects other magic. Apparently it's rare, and if Exitium wanted it, most likely that's what Vincent was going after as well. But for what, I'm not sure," Adam said. Julie looked up, remembering her own conversation with Vin.

"Wait! He told me something. He said he knew someone who got sent to the MSF facility and escaped it. That person couldn't use their powers anymore, like they were taken from them. Could Exitium's boss have something that could do that too?" She asked. Clay was anxiously waiting for some sort of solution and plan of action.

"I'm not sure, but it's a possibility. For now, we need to focus on one thing at a time right now, getting Albert back. And I believe I have an idea of how we can find them," Adam said.

✦ ✦ ✦ ✦ ✦

"Nothing here," Ruby said into the radio from the top of the South mountain.

"No clues out East," Wyndham called out from the edge of the valley.

"Nothing to the North," Adam said from the North Mountain. There was hesitation from the radio before one last response.

"No sign of them at the geysers," Lupos replied to the radio.

"Alright, let's regroup. We'll meet at the edge of the forest. I'll have a group escort the Tarrenians to Brakata while I, Lupos and a team of Red Hand keep searching for the other two," Vale commanded, the group all being transported back to the edge of the forest. Clay immediately approached Vin, who took a step back as Clay got in his face.

"Are you sure you didn't see anything near the geysers?" He asked, remembering Carter's words before he died. Vin looked at Lupos for a second, hesitating before he replied.

"Look, I think we found a lead. But we need to get you guys out of the country before the MSF catches up with us. I can promise you we'll find your brother," Vin said.

"Promise on your mother's grave you'll bring him back to me," Clay said, stepping forward, balling his fists up.

"Alright… I promise on my mother's grave… and yours," Vale said. Clay stepped back, sighing and holding his head for a second in concern for Albert.

The group was transported by Adam to the roof of Titan Squad HQ, looking over the border and the bridge that ran across the trench.

"It's quieter than usual out here," Clay noted as he looked to the border, crossing his arms. Julie stood beside him, putting a hand on his shoulder as they both immediately looked around the land for Double Users, as they had done the last time they stood there.

"I have a guy who can create some fake ID's for you three, and Albert & Vincent once they join you. I'll get you in contact with him and once we know where we are on the map, I'll get you directions for where to go to get to the Haven. That's where most of our friends and family are on the surface," Vin said, cracking his knuckles as he looked over the trench for any security that would stop them from crossing.

"Why don't you just send all the Magic Users in Tarren that way to keep them safe from the MSF?" Clay asked.

"Same reason we attacked your brother during the Goldberg attack. We don't know how many Magic Users there are in Tarren. There isn't exactly a record of it," Vin replied. Looking to the trench and the remnants of the explosion made by the Wild One that Titan Squad fought. Clay looked at Vale a moment, raising an eyebrow.

"You never did tell us why you even attacked there. I think a random genocide would be something that at least deserves an explanation," Clay said, turning to Vin.

"Alright, look. I'll explain. But just understand that I know what I did, what I made everyone else do, was wrong. All of it was. That attack should never have happened," Vin said, putting a knee on the ledge of the building and sighing.

"I was raised by a good family. My father was strong but caring. My mother was as kind as you could ask for. But after my Father got sick, my Mother went to the s–" Vale paused, "to Tarren, looking for a doctor who could help him. Well, she told a doctor all the symptoms he was having were happening to her, hoping he'd give her some medicine, but instead, they took her to the hospital. After some blood tests, they figured out she was a Magic User. It was six days before I came looking for her, and after talking to the doctors she went to and claiming I was her friend, I made my way to Rotun and the MSF facility. I... I watched them take her power. A Magic-User was there, working with the MSF, who had the ability to take people's abilities. He took her flames, and then they executed her. The Red Hand and I had already been attacking military installations to try and weaken them so that when we made our sanctuary here, it wouldn't be contested as heavily by the military. But when I saw her blood stain the floor of that building..." Vin said, pausing a moment and wiping tears from his eyes.

"I lost it. We made a plan to attack the MSF facility. A large group and I would attack some random town close enough to the Capital to send a response but far enough away that they wouldn't be back in time if our plan worked. But I didn't want to just cause some chaos... I wanted to kill them all. Every single person who called themselves 'normal' up here, when their government uses our own against us like that, and for that man to be as vile as to take people's powers and leave them for dead... I don't know how many Wild Ones, how many of us he's taken powers away from, but it's too many, I know," Vin said. Clay looked down, thinking.

"I think Albert has felt the same way over the last eight months that you did at that moment," Clay said.

"I guess I don't have to say it, but be careful getting through that forest. Brakata has a… habit… of taking hordes of Wild Ones and herding them into Tarren," Vin said, pointing to the edge of the tree line. Clay nodded, looking at Adam, who crossed his arms.

"We know all about the Wild Ones, though we're not sure as to why or where they're coming from," Adam said, looking back over the trenches along the border. As he looked further down, he narrowed his eyes, now deep in thought.

"It's strange… Usually, we see hordes of Wild Ones fighting with MSF soldiers day and night here. But the fields to the West are empty," Adam said, rubbing his chin for a moment. Clay raised his head up, realizing what Adam had said.

"Oh yeah, I guess I got used to the distant gunfire after a while at the HQ. I wonder where everything is?" Clay asked, his brow furrowing.

A loud boom echoed in the far distance, a plume of black smoke beginning to flow into the air from the other side of the trees, in Brakata.

"There, something's going on… Clay. You usually keep up with the news, has anything been said about Brakata lately?" Adam asked. Clay pulled out his phone, checking the news.

"Yeah, apparently the Chancellor addressed the whole situation in Rotun already," Clay said, playing a video of the speech. Vin looked over before Lupos called him over for the two of them to discuss plans on finding Albert and Vincent.

"-Yesterday, the Red Hand launched an attack on the Heart of Tarren, our Capital, and as a result, 26 brave soldiers from the Magic Suppression Force gave their lives. The Red Hand, along with some new recruits to their ranks, attacked a convoy of trucks, and attempted to bring wholesale destruction to the city around them. Although there were no civilian casualties, this latest attack is the last that I will allow Tarren to witness. No more shall this nation be held hostage by fear of these Magic Users, and no more will they wreak havoc in our cities. As of today, I am declaring a state of emergency within Tarren, and enacting Martial law, in order to root out these Magic Users and take them down,"

Clay, Adam and Julie all listened intently.

"I am also adding five new names to the Red Hand's members we have files on. However, unlike most of the Red Hand's members, these five were born and raised on Tarren soil, living amongst the citizens. Clay and Albert Barrett, Adam Vander Esch, Vincent Johnson, and Julie Alvarez. All five were at one time Tarren Citizens, but they are now terrorists seeking to destroy our peace. And the worst part is, they may not be the only ones,"

As the Chancellor continued on, clearly trying to incite fear and suspicion of citizens against their neighbors, Clay sighed, looking back to the tree line.

"But what's this all about? He never even mentioned Brakata…" Clay said, thinking.

"We believe that the Red Hand has been operating out of a few sites within the nation of Brakata, to our South. We are currently mobilizing a special military operation to root out the Magic Users and bring them back into Tarren, along with a few occupations of the sites we believe the Red Hand are using, in an attempt to ambush them when they return to the sites," Chancellor Ambrose said.

"Vin!" Clay called, turning his phone off and stopping the video. As Vin walked over, Clay repeated what Ambrose said to him.

"They're going after our Sanctuary sites? That's insane! The Brakata military must be fighting back already," He said, turning to face the plume of smoke.

"Unless they don't know Tarren's already coming," Vin said, furrowing his brow and looking at Clay and Adam.

"Alright, we'll, I know you two said you don't want to join our cause, but we could use some help before we get you asylum. Can you manage that?" Vin asked.

It was dark.

Vincent turned on an electric lantern that he had grabbed earlier, and now that they had turned a corner and sunlight no longer shone on them, it was pitch black in front of them besides the small radius of light that Vincent now held. The two walked down the small tunnel in front of them, walls of rock seemingly forced apart more than carved surrounding them.

"You said this was the Red Hand's home?" Albert asked, cracking his knuckles.

"Not just their home… the home of them, the Double Users, and a whole lot more. Even where I was born and raised," Vincent replied. Albert's brow furrowed as he thought over what Vincent had said.

"Wait, you're not originally from Tarren?" He said, confused.

"No, I didn't go to Tarren until I was about 20, about last year," Vincent said.

Soon enough, the two came to an opening, a multitude of lights below them as they approached a doorway, leading out to a small balcony with winding stairs that led towards the source of the lights.

"Albert… welcome to the Ark,"

Titan Squad and the Red Hand quickly moved into the forest, towards the source of the smoke. It took them a while to plan out their next moves, and by the time they made it past the trees, a small town that they approached was already in ruin.

Clay, Adam and Julie moved to the town, headed towards Main Street as the Red Hand searched for wherever the Tarrenian Army went.

As the three entered the town, they saw burned vehicles, bits of wood and debris all over the roads, which were wet with motor oil, blood and water from a few hydrants that were broken. Bodies littered the road and sidewalks, only a couple of them actually armed. Most seemed to be civilians, but were gunned down, burned, and flattened all the same. The stench of death filled the air, followed closely by the smell of charred flesh. It was enough to make Julie vomit, which she did as they walked through the road, Clay stopping to hold her hair and rub her back as Adam took a look at the carnage.

"I understand their prejudice towards Magic Users, but this… this is just murder," Adam said, looking at a female body, parts of its legs scorched down to the bone and one of its arms sticking up in the air, bent at the elbow.

In the middle of the street, a corpse dressed in a military uniform lay face down with his rifle beside him, the chamber empty and the trigger stuck on the body's hand.

"This definitely wasn't too recent… most of the fighting is already over. I wonder what that plume of smoke was…?" Adam asked, rubbing his chin in thought. A loud boom, as if from a cannon, echoed throughout the town, and overhead, a white light beamed across the sky, deeper into Brakata territory.

"Artillery fire. Perhaps Tarren forces were closer to HQ than we thought?" Adam said while

Clay watched the round fly off into the distance. Julie slowly recovered from her vomiting, standing straight again.

"We can't… let them push into Brakata. It's a sovereign nation. They have no reason to invade like this," Julie said. Adam nodded, crossing his arms.

Clay looked down at his radio, thinking for a moment.

"Hey guys, maybe we can figure out their moves through their frequency? Do you know what the usual frequency is that the infantry use?" Clay asked, while Adam thought for a moment.

"If you turn to frequency 248.1, I think you should pick up some chatter," Adam said.

Nodding, Clay turned his radio, hearing mostly static but soon picking up a couple of voices.

"-don't need some scandal about war crimes going around. Level the buildings. We'll claim the Magic Users did it. Just make sure our reinforcements clean up any of our munitions that don't go off," A woman's voice commanded.

"Yes, sir. We have a bearing and are ready to fire all weapons," A man replied.

"Fire at will. All our forces are evacuated," The woman spoke again.

Clay's eyes widened and he looked up to Adam and Julie, who both were looking at the radio in shock for a second. Above them, a group of four planes flew over them, headed further South into Brakata territory.

"Clay, radio in to the Red Hand on our frequency! We need to get out of the area!" Adam said, looking down the road and opening a portal before gently grabbing Julie, Clay following behind as the three went through, exiting just outside of town and looking back to it as Clay reached the Titan Squad frequency.

"Vin, Lupos, everyone get Chris to get you out of there! They're gonna-"

Before Clay could finish his sentence, a flurry of loud explosions was heard, about 20 in the span of 5 seconds. Above them, they could see a trail of smoke leading into the air, and the sound of metal whistling in the wind.

A+n artillery shell slammed into the middle of town, the first of several that came crashing down on the town. In seconds, 20 shells exploded upon buildings, streets, and everything in between. Clay and Titan Squad couldn't see where the Red Hand was, but there was an ominous silence over the radio.

Nobody was answering.

Nobody spoke.

Nobody did anything for a moment.

"Lupos… come in. Are you there? Is anyone hurt?" Clay asked.

Clay waited for 5 seconds.

Then 10 seconds.

Silence.

"Lupos? Ruby? Vin? Anyone?" Clay asked again.

He waited 5 seconds…

"Clay! We got out, but Vin didn't. Chris got him out last, and he's already worse for ware. We're picking you up, is everyone on your side okay?" Lupos finally replied. Clay breathed a sigh of relief, as did Adam and Julie.

"We're fine. How's Vin?" Clay asked. Julie vanished into a cloud of smoke.

"We'll have to show you when you get here," Lupos replied. Adam vanished as well, before Clay was transported to the edge of the forest near town, about half a mile along the forest from where they already were.

The Red Hand were licking their wounds, a few of them in line to get patched up by the Double User they had picked up in Rotun. However, as Clay saw Ruby and Tristan kneeling beside Vin, a bit of confusion crossed his face.

"What happened? Is he already patched up?" Clay asked. Lupos looked up at him, a nervous look on his face.

"His wounds were already healed, but something's wrong. I think he had some kind of out-of-body experience, so while he's still breathing, it's like he went into a coma. We're not sure if he's gonna pull through, especially without any hospitals out here," Tristan said, looking back down at Vin.

As they sat for a moment, Clay kneeled beside Lupos, looking briefly at Ruby, who sat holding Vin's hand, tears in her eyes. While he felt compelled to say something, to comfort her, he knew nothing he could say would do much, especially with the uncertainty of Vin's situation.

"Well, we patched into a Tarren military frequency. Apparently they're moving through the area with reinforcements soon to clean the town up and blame the civilian deaths on Magic Users," Clay explained as Lupos turned his attention to him.

"So, most likely we need to stop those reinforcements from helping the men on the front line?" Lupos asked.

"And probably keep them from touching the scene they created, so that if by chance any reporters or journalists come to town, they'll see it was Tarren's military that destroyed the town and not us," Clay said. Lupos nodded, bringing a clawed hand up to rub his chin a bit.

"So does that mean we need to go easy on them to show we're not a threat to Tarren's citizens?" Lupos asked.

"No... it means we need to hit them fast and hard, so they don't have a chance to react," Clay said, looking down, a hesitant look on his face.

"I'm surprised you're able to say such things when you were just fighting alongside those soldiers a couple of days ago," Lupos said.

"I am too... but it wasn't me or Titan Squad who traded sides. Chancellor Ambrose betrayed us, so we can't hesitate to fight back, no matter how much I want to. Plus, what they're doing here is wrong. None of us would agree to do this to other people, no matter who gave the order," Clay replied, looking back to the town, ensuring his radio was secure on his belt. Military comms continued chattering back and forth as Clay readied his rifle, taking a breath to prepare himself. Lupos stood as well, looking back to the town, crossing his arms.

"Alright, what's the plan?"

Vale opened his eyes, looking up into the clear blue sky above. He felt weightless. Nothing about him felt real anymore...

He slowly stood, looking all around. The world was in a haze, but it looked like he was in some sort of field, his vision limited by a white fog.

From the fog, he saw a figure, a female approaching. He tended up for just a moment, before he was able to make out who it was.

Vale's mother, who had the same black hair as him. She stepped towards him, a smile on her face.

"Vin… I've waited for a long time to see you again," She said. Behind her, a brown-haired man walked up, his silver eyes nearly piercing through Vin's body.

"It's good to see you again, son," The man, Vin's father, said.

Vin looked at both of them before falling to his knees, shaking and putting his head down, tears filling his eyes.

"I can't… I can't be here yet…" he said. His mother kneeled down in front of him, wrapping her arms around his shoulders.

"I know, you want to atone for everything. I'm sorry you didn't get the chance," His mother said. His dad kneeled down behind him, putting a hand on his shoulder.

"You did a lot of good for our people, Vin. But you hurt a lot of others," Vin's dad said.

"I know… I'm sorry. I'm so sorry," Vale replied, sobbing into his mother's arm.

"We know you are, son," His mother replied, stroking his hair.

"We need to go," His father said.

"But I have to go back. Tristan, Ruby, the others, they-" Vin said, trying to stand before his father put a hand on his shoulder, giving him a stern look.

"Vin. They're gonna be fine. I promise," He said before smiling.

Vin and his mother both stood, each of his parents taking his hands as they began walking forward, Vin looking back one last time before the three of them continued, fading into the white expanse…

A convoy of 3 tanks and 8 soldiers walked down the road towards town, six of the soldiers in formation in front of the three tanks, with two more men taking up the rear of the convoy to spot enemies. Their ballistic masks covered their faces, and the way they walked, it seemed like their equipment had taken its toll on them, between their vests, masks, rifles and other equipment.

Clay and Chris were in a tall tree overlooking the road, watching the convoy and preparing to start their attack. Ruby, Julie, Lupos and Adam were near the front of the convoy, hidden behind the woods, while Zoe and the bat twins were further down, all within the trees spread out, with Zoe near the back of the convoy.

"Looks like everything is in position. Watch the back of the convoy. Once I transport the first man away, it's go time. Remember to use the tanks' blind spots," Chris said to his communicator. Clay's radio was emitting the same voice as everyone else's, only at a higher volume.

Clay hopped down from the tree after giving Chris a quick nod.

One of the soldiers in the back of the convoy was enveloped in a cloud of smoke, which also appeared just in front of Clay. He brought his rifle up, seeing the confused soldier look around before he pressed the barrel of his gun to the back of the soldier's head.

"Drop the rifle. Hands up," Clay blankly said, the soldier slowly complying. However, before he could give any more orders, the soldier ducked to the side, turning and grabbing Clay's rifle just as he fired a shot off into the woods. The two struggled for the weapon, falling to the ground over it. Clay was on his back, keeping hold of the grip of the gun. He balled up his fist and sent it to the side of the soldier's neck, knocking him to the side. He rolled over, pulling on his rifle and putting a knee in the soldier's chest. He finally ripped the gun away from the man's grasp, aiming again at him. The soldier put his hands up, slowly moving one towards his chin.

Just as the first soldier disappeared and the second looked over and reached for his communicator, Zoe jumped into the road, sending a metal fist square into the middle of the soldier's mask. He fell back, slammed into the ground, and was knocked unconscious. Zoe looked to the back tank, grabbing a track and yanking it to the side, partially off its wheels.

Ruby sent rock spires into the bottom of all three tanks, ripping through the metal plates underneath and stopping them all in their tracks.

Adam threw a portal out in the trees across the path, hidden behind the leaves. Julie sent out a group of 8 figures, all of them rising from the dirt beneath the soldiers. The soldiers were panicked, firing at the men who did little more than flinch at the bullets slamming into them.

Lupos and Adam ran onto the road, Lupos running through and using his claws to cut down the men wherever he could, be it the throat, the arms, or just below the vests in the lower abdomen.

The tanks tried to aim down at Lupos, but as he ducked underneath one of the barrels, the front tank aimed at Adam. With no machine gun on the top of them, and the crew seemingly too scared to open their top hatch and face Adam themselves, they aimed the barrel right at him. However, Adam stood his ground, putting a hand out in front of him and waiting.

The tank fired just as Adam opened a portal in front of him. The shell soared through the portal, and from the trees, the shell slammed into the side of the tank, through the armor, and into the ammo rack. Explosion after explosion blew from the inside of the tank, throwing shrapnel and flames all over. Adam kept the portal open, so anything that went his way went back to the tank, and Lupos got down, under the front of the tank, and hoped none of the shrapnel blew out underneath it at him.

As the battle continued, the healing Double User sat back against a tree, away from the fighting, with Vin's body lying beside her. She looked down, her brow furrowing as she looked to her hands. She was shaking.

Clay froze as he watched the soldier pull his mask off. He stared into the eyes of the soldier who had once helped him through boot camp…

Parks was on the ground, at the wrong end of Clay's rifle barrel.

"Clay…? what are you doing here?" Parks asked, catching his breath for a moment. Clay slowly lowered his gun, aiming it at the dirt below them.

"Parks, I…" Clay trailed off, looking down.

"You're with the Red Hand? Albert said they killed your family," Parks said, confusion on his face, "Why would you be helping them?" He asked. Clay took a moment of hesitation before he responded.

"I'm not helping them because I like them. But what the Chancellor, what Tarren is doing, it's wrong," Clay replied.

"So you're just gonna kill your friends to stop it? Brakata is harboring terrorists. You can't–" Parks started before Clay interrupted.

"They're not terrorists! And neither am I. Albert and I just wanted to save J-… Sergeant Alvarez and Vander Esch," Clay said.

"The Chancellor was gonna kill them? Why?" Parks said, sitting up with his hands resting on the ground and holding him up.

"I don't know. We were trying to figure out where the Wild Ones were coming from, but-"

The second tank exploded just as the first, causing both of them to flinch before facing each other again.

"I can't explain everything. But I'm still your friend, Parks. I don't want to go to war against you or Tarren. But the Chancellor is up to something," He said, walking towards his old friend.

"Wait, what are you doing?" Parks asked, trying to stand.

Clay pulled his rifle back, slamming the butt of the gun into the side of Parks' head, knocking him out cold. After making sure he wasn't bleeding, Clay ran to join the others just as the third tank had its hatch opened, Zoe jumping inside. Gunfire rang out briefly, and the crew of the tank screamed, but once it fell silent, Zoe climbed back out of the tank.

"That's the whole convoy. We can just hope Brakata pushes the front line soldiers back now," Lupos said, looking back at the group of soldiers in the front torn apart, one of them leaning on another body, slumped over.

"Hold on, I hear something," Lupos said, walking down the road, Clay and Zoe following as Adam looked over the bodies as well.

It was only a whisper, but Lupos picked up the noise.

"We need a bombing run on the road, section 119286," the soldier whispered between pained breaths, "Several Red Hand members in the area, our squad was wiped out... rain fire," The soldier whispered. Lupos grabbed the man and picked him up off the ground, causing him to yell and drop the radio that sat connected to the dead body he leaned on.

"That was a bad idea," Lupos said. The soldier looked at him defiantly.

"I'm dead already. At least I'll take a few of you to hell with me," He said, pulling a dampener from his pocket and slapping it on Lupos' arm, wrapping his own arm around it to keep them from removing it.

Lupos backed up, Clay raising his rifle and shooting the man, who while mostly limp, still hung on to Lupos' arm.

"C'mon, we have to get it off him before the fire drops! He won't be able to transport!" Clay yelled, pulling out his knife as Lupos fell to a knee, balling his fist and punching the soldier. He held his grip still.

As Clay ran up, trying to pry the man's arms off Lupos, the group heard the artillery guns firing, and the whistles of shells flying into the air. Everyone at that point had gathered in the road to help get the man and the dampener off Lupos, and Adam had opened a portal for them all. However, as Clay felt another sense of deja vu, he paused, looking up at the artillery shells, which now sat in mid-air, just above the treeline.

Something was reaching for him.

Vin was sitting at a table with his parents in their old house, tears in his eyes as he explained his actions. The house itself was just like everything else. Mostly everything was white, besides some of the furniture and some decorations on the walls. Vale had traded in his old clothes for a white robe, the same as what his parents both wore.

"Once we had our sanctuaries in Brakata, we wanted to," he said, pausing and looking behind him quickly, as if something was standing behind him.

"Vin? What's wrong?" His mother asked. Vin looked down for a moment before turning his attention back to his parents.

"I don't know… it feels like something is coming after me, or someone. Like I'm being stalked," He said. His parents both looked at one another with concerned expressions.

"What? What is it?" He asked.

"Did any of your friends from the Earth have a necromancy power?" His mother asked.

◆◆◆◆◆

As Clay and the others looked at the shells, the sound of a single pair of footsteps approached. They were heavy and metal, like a knight in armor.

Clay looked down the road a bit and saw Exitium, alone, with his hand raised halfway, walking towards the group. Clay tensed immediately, knowing he was basically useless in a fight against this guy.

"Lupos. Grab Vin and get your asses back to the Ark. You all have done enough damage as it is," Exitium said. Lupos looked down, sighing as Clay finally removed his dampener. While it didn't change his appearance, the Red Hand knew the man had just stuck it there so they couldn't transport him away the same way they did the others. Though, if Exitium had not arrived, Clay also knew they had Adam's portal and could have brought Vin and the healer with Chris' ability.

"Tarren is invading Brakata. We can't just sit here and let it happen!" Lupos said, walking towards Exitium.

"The affairs of these people are none of our concern. As long as the Ark is not discovered, none of this is our business," Exitium replied. Lupos sighed, rubbing his head.

"Fine. We'll go back for now. But we still have to protect our sanctuaries. If Tarren gets near them…" Lupos said.

"Bring them to the Ark if it needs to be. Assuming they're not Double Users, they can live peacefully there," Exitium said.

With a curse under his breath, Lupos nodded and looked back to Chris.

"Let's get back home," Lupos reluctantly said. Chris nodded, looking into the woods for a while.

"Hold on!" Clay exclaimed, Lupos and Exitium looking at him.

"We've fought you twice trying to keep you from dragging Albert and me to who knows where, why the hell would we go with you now?" Clay asked.

"I will not argue with you after you and your team caused Lance to be executed. If you would like, I could allow the Red Hand to leave and let go of these shells on my way out," Exitium said. Clay looked up again at the 20 or so artillery shells above their heads and sighed.

"Fine. I'll go," Clay said, looking back to Julie and Adam.

"If you're going, I'm coming with you," Julie said, putting a hand on Clay's shoulder.

"This may be the piece of the puzzle we're missing in this whole situation. Let's gather information and learn what we can while we're there," Adam said, putting his hand on Clay's other shoulder.

"I'll bring Vin and the old lady back first. We'll be right behind," Chris said. He quickly waved his hand, both of them disappearing before each member of the Red Hand, along with the Three of Titan Squad and Exitium, all disappeared, and the shells slammed into the ground where they once stood.

Chapter 8

＊✦◆✦＊

Vin felt a cold hand wrap around his torso. It pulled him from his house despite his struggle, grabbing anything he could in a vain attempt to stay. He was pulled from the world he was in, sucked back into his body, and as he opened his eyes, a shock of pain, sorrow, and anger flooded over him.

Vin screamed, sitting up and looking around for a moment. He was in a bed, in what seemed like a Clemencian hospital. The equipment was outdated, mostly nothing more than IV's, syringes and counters full of all kinds of drugs from Ammonia to Sulfadiazine.

Looking over himself, Vin realized he was among the living again. Several different emotions flooded through him for a moment, before his head settled on one thought that pushed them all back down.

"I'm not done here, yet," Vin thought. As upset as he was, he couldn't go back now, no matter how much he wanted to. The last thing any of the Red Hand wanted to do was see him suicided.

Vin slowly stood, his legs wobbly and unbalanced, causing him to lean on the bed as he struggled to walk. He made his way to the wall that the door was in, opening the door and listening in to the hall outside.

"Well, whether she did it or not, we're lucky. We still need him, some of us more than others," He heard Lupos say.

"Well, before I say anything, me and the others need to see what this place really is. We never really got an explanation to what this 'Ark' is all about," Clay said.

Vin stepped into the hall, turning his head and seeing the two talk, Julie and Adam standing beside Clay.

"First off, where, exactly, are we?" Adam asked.

"Look, I'll answer all your questions in a moment. For now, I want to see if Vin is- ...awake yet," Lupos was saying, pausing as he saw Vin leaning on the wall in the hallway.

"Alright, back to bed. You're still recovering," Lupos said, walking towards Vin while the three Titan Squad members followed. As he reached for Vin, he slapped his hand away, flames erupting over half his face as he looked at Lupos, another fire in his eyes that burned brighter than the flames on his cheek and neck.

"Who brought me back?! I was just fine where I was!" He yelled. Lupos put his hands out towards Vin to calm him down.

"Alright, hey, calm down. That Double User we found with you in Rotun was a necromancer. She brought you back," Lupos said.

"Where the hell is she?!" He snapped.

"Well..." Lupos said, rubbing his neck. Adam sighed, crossing his arms.

"She committed suicide in her bunk last night," He said.

"Last night? Wait... how long have I been out?" Vin asked.

"About three days. But the lady told us what she did, so we put you in a bed and waited for you to come back," Lupos said. Vin looked out the window for a moment, narrowing his eyes.

"Are we...?" He asked.

"We're back in the Ark, yes. And because they're not fighting with Tarren anymore, we have three new members," Lupos said.

"Hey, who said we were members?!" Julie spoke up, so far simply listening and taking in information until now. She walked up to Lupos, nose to nose with the beast.

"Let me make something clear. We aren't trying to join your weird PMC bullshit. We want the Tarren people to accept what we are, and we want to go home, as soon as we know we won't be killed there," Julie said.

"Oh, really?" Lupos said, raising his eyebrows and leaning forward, bringing their noses even closer, "Well how do you expect to do that when nearly every politician and news outlet in the country is fear mongering and using us as a way to keep your 'people' scared and obedient?" He asked.

Julie paused, looking down before stepping back in a huff.

"Well, I understand your point, but I still don't like the idea of joining with you guys and your reputation," Julie said.

"You mean the reputation we got from those same news outlets and politicians that are probably calling you all traitors and villains now?" He asked, Julie's eyes widening once she realized.

"Alright, you've made your point," She said, defeated. Vin sighed, rubbing his forehead.

"Maybe it's a good thing that I got yanked back," He said, leaning more on the wall. Lupos ducked his head under one of Vin's arms and helped him back towards his bed.

"Well, until your body is ready to exercise again, you need to rest. We'll get you some food, get you rested up, with some actual sleep, and get you ready to go again," Lupos said. Vin sighed, the flames on his face going out as he nodded.

"Yeah… that sounds good. I'm tired, even though it feels like I just woke up," Vin replied.

Adam, Julie and Clay walked through the hall of the hospital, noticing the place was mostly barren. Adam rubbed his chin, thinking.

"The Ark… we haven't really gotten the chance to see much of this place yet," He said.

"Yeah, come to think of it, where has Exitium been? It's been three days and we haven't seen anything but darkness outside, and Exitium is nowhere," Adam said. Julie and Clay nodded in agreement, Clay's brow furrowing.

"You guys remember when Carter said that in school it was always pitch balance outside?" Julie asked, her mind wandering. Clay nodded, looking back to her.

"I was thinking the same thing. Do you think Carter used to be in the Ark?" Clay asked, Adam nodding as well.

"That would explain a lot. But if that's the case, in what you two told me, he said it was dark for years for him. So, do you think that we're now anywhere near where he was stuck in darkness?" Adam asked. Clay walked to the window, looking up towards the sky.

"I wish I had a flashlight. I wanna know what's up there. I don't see any stars, so there has to be some sort of ceiling, right?" Clay said.

"I'm sure there is. But it's too dark to see any walls or anything, so how can we know how big this place is? We don't even know where on a map it is, we could be in some unmarked spot off the coast," Julie said.

"No," Adam said, crossing his arms, "We're still within Brakata's borders. The humidity hasn't changed, if we were out to sea, we'd know it. The air wouldn't be this dry,"

Clay thought for a moment, looking down as he put the pieces together.

"Do you guys think this place is where Albert and Vincent went?" Clay asked. Julie and Adam both went silent for a moment.

"There's a lot about Vincent we don't know. Julie and I have known each other since we were young, but Vincent, he only joined the team a year ago. Neither of us heard too much about his past life, just that he was raised in a rich part of his town," Adam said. Clay nodded, looking back to the window.

"Well, I guess all we can do is wait. I don't like putting our fate in others' hands, especially Exitium's, after all we've gone through, but what other choice do we have now?" Clay asked.

"We could always grab a few lights and try to find Albert ourselves?" Julie suggested.

"I doubt we'll have any luck. The building is sealed tight, and even if we did leave, with as dark as it is outside, we'd get lost in moments. There must be another part to this place, wherever Carter said he went to school. It must have been in some kind of town here, we just can't see it," Adam said.

Metal footsteps approached the three of them, causing them all to tense up. Turning, they faced Exitium, still wary about his intentions.

"My apologies for the strange spot to bring you these last few days. Just wanted to make sure you weren't planning on harming any of our citizens while I was away," Exitium said, resting his arms on the waistband of his armor.

"I was gonna say this was pretty underwhelming of a place. Is this really the Ark?" Clay asked.

"Not exactly. We're close, but not inside the Ark yet. Now that I know you are all cooperative, we'll bring you inside the Ark and show you around before taking you to meet our leader. He'll be very excited to hear three more have entered the Ark, especially a descendent of Arnold Lewis," Exitium said. Julie looked to Clay, speaking with a hushed voice.

"Who's Arnold Lewis?" She whispered.

"I'm not sure, but I think he's the first one who had my and Albert's power. Exitium and Lance called me 'Lewis' before, too," Clay said. Julie nodded as Adam spoke to Exitium.

"So if we haven't entered the Ark yet, what's outside this building?" Adam asked.

"We sealed this building for a good reason. Outside is nothing but hordes of Double Users. Most of them are violent and insane, so we don't allow them to see. That way, they can't hurt one another, or find their way back into the Ark," Exitium said. Adam nodded, looking back outside.

"So, what is the ceiling and the walls? There's no sun or moonlight coming in, si aren't we in some sort of structure?" Adam asked. Exitium said nothing, looking out the window a second before turning around.

"Let me know when you are all ready. I'll make sure the Red Hand is prepared to leave," Exitium said, walking away without another word. Adam narrowed his eyes, once again reminded not to trust these men.

The group was transported to a long hallway, darkness behind them and a gate in front of them, light seeping through the spaces between the wood and metal that made up the gate. All of them walked towards the light, Exitium raising his hand and in turn raising the wood, letting them enter the huge city within.

"This is the Ark," Exitium said, Clay and Julie looking in awe of the city.

Buildings as far as the eye could see, people of all shapes and sizes, with all different kinds of magic abilities walking around, talking, and in the middle of town, a market, with stone stands lining the street. Nearly every house was made completely of stone or brick, not a single piece of wood used anywhere.

The three of them looked on in amazement, Clay and Julie slowly walking towards the market, while Adam sat behind with Exitium.

"Is this entire city under this roof?" He asked, looking up. Around the gate, walls stretched all the way up to the ceiling, connecting to it.

"Yes, it is. The Ark was created as a safe haven for Magic Users near the end of the second Great War. A group of earth-based users created every building you see here, every wall and road," Exitium replied as the two of them slowly walked forward, trailing behind Clay and Julie, who were looking over what was being sold by the market merchants. It was mostly small numbers of vegetables and meats, obviously all localized and none of it industrial or mass produced.

"So, I assume there's limited agriculture here due to the environment?" Adam said, raising an eyebrow at Exitium.

"We have a space reserved for food production. That area gets a fair amount of sunlight, but we have an… agreement with Brakata. They've provided us with the means for electricity and we've bought heat lamps from them that allow some of the families of government officials to grow their own food as well," Exitium briefly explained. Adam nodded, crossing his arms.

"So, food isn't an issue here, then. Interesting," He said, looking around a moment. Beef, pork and chicken all being sold, some of it raw for the buyer to cook, and some of it cooked and sold as a meal instead.

"As for a water source?" Adam asked.

"There's a freshwater river that runs underneath the wall briefly. It's up to water-based Magic Users to cleanse it and make it drinkable. We also have a sewer system that leads into it downstream from where it passes through town," Exitium explained. Adam nodded, still looking around.

"So, it seems like this place is nearly perfect. But…" he thought, Exitium looked at him as he found his point.

"A lack of children. Double Users must not be smiled upon here," Adam said.

"That… is our biggest issue, for the most part," Exitium said, "Without non-Magic Users to bear children with, not only is there a lack of children, but bloodlines will soon end. There are rumors of some sort of black market on Tarrenians and Brakatans, but of course, that's highly illegal and the government is currently working on rooting out the trafficking rings," Exitium said, hooking his thumbs onto his belt.

"That… awful," Adam said, furrowing his brow and looking down.

"Though, I understand the cause. We've seen all too much how Wild Ones can become violent for seemingly no reason. What happens when a couple has a Double User child?" Adam asked.

"The child is given an aptitude test when they turn 16. If they're deemed safe by the government, they're allowed to stay within the Ark unless they commit a violent crime. If they are deemed dangerous, they are sent out of the Ark, to the darkness outside. There's nothing but scraps out there, and I personally hate that we treat people that way, but I have no say in the matter," Exitium said. Adam shook his head.

"That's terrible. Back at the lab in Tarren, our goal was to help the Wild Ones we captured from the border near Brakata," Adam said.

"Well, I believe the King's policy is out of panic. The issue of Double Users is only a recent occurrence. When the Magic Users were brought to the Ark, there was a large number of non-users brought in from Clemence as well, but now that the new generation is growing to age, most of the non-Magic Users are either dead or had Magic-User children. Nobody knew what would happen with two Magic Users, seeing as less than one percent of the original Magic Users were women," Exitium said. The two of them reached the end of the market, and Clay and Julie stopped to buy some fried chicken from one of the merchants.

"Hey, what the heck is this?" The merchant asked as Clay tried to hand him his money.

"What? It's like 10 bucks, that should cover it, right?" He asked.

"Yeah, if we were in Tarren! That stuff is useless out here!" The merchant said, looking down the road.

"Guards! This guy has Tarrenian money!" The merchant yelled. Julie and Clay backed up, now shaken and unsure of what to do.

Exitium turned, walking over to them and turning his head to the merchant.

"They're with me," He said, reaching into his back pocket and pulling out a wallet, taking out a brown slip of paper and handing it over.

"Oh, sorry about that, didn't know. You know how those black market guys can be," The Merchant said, taking the money and setting the chicken on the counter.

Exitium waved for the two of them to follow him, approaching Adam again.

"This place has its fair share of problems. But Tarren is hardly an issue here. The citizens are mostly happy and the government is fair," Exitium said. Adam nodded and walked with him again while Clay and Julie observed the city as they walked and ate.

"So, why bring us here? I assume you wanted Clay's power here for a reason," Adam said.

"That's true. However, we wanted you and Ms. Alvarez to come, as well," Exitium said.

"You know our names?" Adam said, raising an eyebrow.

"We have ears everywhere. Gathering information about Magic Users in Tarren that we can extract before they're killed. And, to complete the Ark," Exitium replied.

"Complete the Ark?" Adam said inquisitively.

"Our goal here is to gather as many of the 100,000 Magic abilities in one place as possible. We're close, but we still must search for the last of those trapped in hostile lands. Speaking of which, Mr. Johnson and the other Barrett brother. Do you know where they are?"

"So, that's why I need your help. Just attend one of these meetings and you'll understand what's happening," Vincent said as he and Albert sat in a hotel room near the capitol building of the Ark. However, Albert clearly seemed distracted from the conversation.

"So, this is where the Magic Users all left to during their Exodus," He said, watching the crowds of people go by.

"Yeah, I almost forgot you knew about the Exodus already," Vincent said, pacing back and forth.

"So why did your King want to capture me and Clay so badly?" Albert asked in a monotone voice.

"Well, see, there's hardly any weapons in the Ark. there's almost no guns or anything. People with combative powers use their abilities to fight, and a decent number of those are in the military police," Vincent said.

"So you want me to be a magic suppressor to catch thieves who can hold their own in a fight," Albert finished his sentence, an irritated expression on his face.

"No, no, nothing like that. Think of it like this. The King can see the future. But if you suppressed his magic powers, from what I read, he wouldn't be able to see past the point you let go of him. I don't know what his ability is or how it works, but when Lewis did it-" Vincent was explaining before Albert interrupted.

"Hold on. You knew who my ancestor was?" He said, stepping towards Vincent and balling up his fists.

"Alright, alright, hey. Yes, I knew after I heard what your power was. But you and Clay are the only Magic Users we've seen that can manipulate other magic abilities! There are a few other meta abilities, but none of them can do what you can. But, without the proper training to access your power's full potential, you'll end up just like Julie and Adam, or like those Red Hand crazies," Vincent explained.

"What are you talking about?" Albert asked, crossing his arms.

✦✦✦✦✦

Sleeping arrangements had been made to house Titan Squad while they were in the Ark. they were given a set of three apartments, but the first night they were there, Julie knocked on Clay's door, wanting to talk.

The apartment was small, one bedroom, one bathroom, with a single room that held the kitchen and living room. Everything was decorated with an old design, the couch was a velvet material, brown, with a strange ridge pattern in the middle of the back. The microwave had a wood pattern on the outside, with a dial timer in the middle and three buttons on the bottom for "START," "STOP," and "LIGHT,"

Julie and Clay sat on the couch, looking out the window at the cityscape beyond, lit only by the lights from the windows and streets.

"So, hear anything new on the news?" Julie asked, turning her attention back to Clay.

"I wish. I don't get any signal out here. There's one wi-fi signal here, but it has a password, so I've been shut out," Clay replied, rubbing his forehead. Julie looked around, her eyes falling upon an FM radio sitting on the kitchen table.

"Well, maybe the radio can pick something up? Shouldn't hurt to try," Julie said. Clay looked over, seeing the radio and nodding.

"Sure. I haven't messed with it since we got in, so worth a shot," Clay said. Julie walked over to the table and sat in one of the chairs, facing the radio, Clay not far behind, sitting in an adjacent chair.

Julie turned up the volume dial first, static humming through the room as she began turning the frequency dial. Eventually, she made out a clear transmission.

"-rrival, the Ark is three steps closer to gathering a Magic Users of every ability and re-establishing Clemence as a sovereign nation, set apart from the modern world. In other news, King Ichabod's Royal Guard infiltrated a suspected safe house of the Black Market ring 'the Black Mass' and secured several suspects, black market items, and a group of six non-Magic-User women," The broadcaster said.

Julie shook her head as she listened, sighing.

"That's awful. People getting abducted from their homes and brought here just to bear children?" Julie said, crossing her arms. Clay nodded, looking down.

"Yeah... but, if people here don't have kids, they're just going to die out. I know that doesn't make it right, but what do they do?" Clay asked. Julie thought for a moment.

"I'm not for sure. I don't know how Brakata feels about Magic Users, but it's not like Tarren would allow anyone to enter this place. If they knew it existed, they would probably storm in and destroy everything here," Julie said, looking out the window again.

Clay looked at her for a second, rubbing his neck.

"I wanted to ask you something," Clay said, looking down for a second. Julie turned back to him with an inquisitive look on her face.

"If we somehow had the chance to go back to Tarren, go back home. Would you want to?" Clay asked. Julie looked down for a second, her brow furrowing as she thought.

"Well, would we still be helping the Double Users out there?" She asked, causing Clay to think for a second as well.

"Let's say no. If you got to live out there, and live a normal life," Clay asked. Julie chuckled a bit.

"Nothing about our lives will ever be normal," Julie said, "But, I have always wanted to do good for other people. Maybe we're here so we can do good for people here?" Julie shrugged as she spoke. Clay nodded, smiling.

"Well, I know it was a confusing road getting here, but hopefully from now on, we'll know who our friends and enemies are," Clay said, chuckling, Julie joining him in laughing over the situation.

"Well, if nothing else, hopefully we can do something about the few issues that they're having here," Julie said.

"Yeah, that'd be good. When we talk to their King, hopefully we get a better grasp on the situation," Clay said.

Down the hall, Adam and Exitium had began speaking again, both of them standing outside the apartment building.

"I suppose I should ask before we get into anything serious involving the King. What are your intentions here, now that you've seen this place?" Exitium asked. Adam stopped for a moment, putting a hand to his chin as he thought.

"For a long time now, I haven't known. During my time in Tarren, I simply helped Julie achieve what she wanted to. I didn't have any goals of my own, I simply wanted to see her achieve her's," Adam said, looking up at the Ceiling of the city.

"And now, since you're here?" Exitium asked.

"Now, there's only one word on my mind. Freedom," Adam said. Exitium crossed his arms, looking out at the city.

"I won't disagree with that. This city could use more freedom. In a way, these people are simply waiting around to die. Without any hope for their children growing up, without ambition, something has to be done," Exitium said. Adam nodded, looking over the city.

"This King you work for… what's his name?" Adam asked. Exitium hesitated.

"King Ichabod," He said. Adam looked over, raising an eyebrow.

"The second or third?" He asked.

"The one and only," Exitium said. Adam froze, his brow furrowing.

"King Ichabod is still alive?" Adam said, in shock.

"He is. The years have not been kind to him, but he is still alive and still in power, with no heir to the throne. You'll see more in the morning," Exitium said.

The next day, Titan Squad, Vin, and Lupos would head to the Capitol Building to meet with King Ichabod.

Albert had spent several days with Vincent in the Ark, out in the slums on the SouthEast end of the city. To their West was the industrial side of town, where most of the factories and tons of smoke bellowed, all of it disappearing into the air towards the ceiling where it seemed to disappear. To the North was the financial district, where most of the news, wealthy businesses, and government buildings stood. And to the NorthWest, was the rich residential area, where most of the more wealthy Magic Users lived and worked. In the rich side of town stood the tallest building in the city, which Albert had heard simply be called "the Spire," and was apparently owned by the Billings family and used as an office and penthouse for their mining business, which Vincent told Albert was the main driving force in expanding the city's walls to make more room for businesses and people, as more Magic Users from Tarren and Brakata were brought to the Ark.

As Albert entered the Spire, Vincent ahead of him, he looked over the room in front of him. Straight forward was a set of three elevators, but in front of them, to the left was a wooden desk, a secretary typing on a typewriter. To the right was a set of couches and a very old television, more wood and drawers than the actual screen, which was turned off.

Before passing any further, Albert stopped Vincent for a moment.

"Alright, tell me. Why is everything here so old? It has felt like I stepped into 1945 again since I've been here," Albert whispered to Vincent.

"Yeah, King Ichabod cut off the city from the world in the 40's, they haven't exactly had access to the same inventions ever since," Vincent replied.

"Have they had nothing invented since then around here?" Albert asked.

"Well yeah, but most of it was based on HVAC," Vincent said before walking in, Albert sighing and following.

"Hi, how May I help you?" The woman at the desk asked.

"Yes, can I have a banana?" Vincent asked in a bit of a hushed voice.

"Of course, can I have your names?" She asked.

"Vincent Johnson and…" Vincent looked to Albert, gesturing for him to tell her his name.

"Albert," he thought for a second, "Albert Lewis,"

The two were directed to an elevator that descended until it reached the basement level, which opened up to a hallway with a pair of guards leaning on each wall, dressed in red shirts and black pants. They both had black ball caps on with a distinct cursive drawn "B" on the front.

Vincent and Albert walked forward, through a set of wooden double doors to a room filled with people conversing, designed almost like a church. Rows of seating taking up most of the room, and tables in front of the seating for papers, and microphones on the table every few feet for the people sitting. The seating led to an elevated stage with a podium on the front. Vincent led Albert to a seat near the back of the room, the two sitting down just as an older man in a suit approached the podium. He wore the same hat as the guards, and his curly white hair surrounded the lower edges of the hat. His right eye was silver, contrasted to the blue in his left, signaling he was most likely blind in his right.

"May I have everyone's attention?" He spoke, his grizzled voice speaking into a microphone through to speakers that caught the attention of everyone in the room, who all promptly sat down and prepared to listen.

"I now call this meeting of the Unified Partisan Organization to order," He said, "We will begin by explaining our goals to those who are here for the first time, and introducing some new faces to the organization,"

"Unified Partisan Organization?" Albert leaned over and whispered to Vincent, who turned and leaned back towards him as well.

"They're the only other ones down here besides the Red Hand trying to change things around here. But they're not as violent as Vale's cronies, and focus more on things here instead of what's happening in Tarren or Brakata," Vincent briefly whispered as the old man organized his papers and got ready to speak again.

"We have all heard the news around the Ark. The human trafficking rings conducted by the Black Mass, the Red Hand's attempts at using hit-and-run attacks on Tarren to somehow establish some sort of 'safe haven' for the descendants of those who didn't join us for the Exodus, and the absolute state of nature that has risen within our society. The Ark is supposed to be a shield to protect us Magic Users from the world's persecution! But how can we feel protected when there are so many dangerous people within our own walls?" The man spoke. Albert scanned the room as he listened, seeing the nods of approval from various men and women sitting around the tables.

"King Ichabod, for too long, has ignored the will of the people! He has refused to let us accept help from Brakata, he has refused to let us see the modern world! Their access to medicine, their communication technology, their liberties! He has refused these things from us, and it's time we took them! We are here to find a way to remove King Ichabod from power and place someone on the throne who will talk to Brakata and let us interact! Let us have a chance at having children that aren't cast out of society!"

The more intense his voice got, the more electric the room felt. The people around the man were inspired by his words, excited for the future.

Except for Albert. He listened more to the words than the tone behind it.

"We will help Brakata fight back against the tyranny of Tarren! Their Chancellor has fought tooth and nail to destroy any of us that shows up in his land! We will make sure they pay for their hatred with as much blood as they have spilled! And we will be a United society, a modern society, and a free society!" The man continued. Albert looked down for a moment, thinking to himself as Vincent clapped, applause soon following, which turned into a standing ovation for the man.

"Ladies and gentleman, my name is Oliver Bellum! And welcome again to this month's meeting of the UPO," The man at the podium said, panting a bit from the excitement as the applause died down and the room began to quiet.

"I'd like to make note of a few names that have joined us this month. First, our own outside man, Vincent Johnson!" Bellum announced, prompting a brief applause. Vincent waved his hand to the crowd, Albert looking around for a second at the people looking back to them.

"Also," Bellum continued, "A new face, brought by Vincent, who grew up in Tarren before discovering his true self and his people! Ladies and gentleman, welcome Mr. Albert Lewis!"

The crowd nearly erupted.

Thunderous applause echoed through the room as Albert whispered to Vincent.

"Why such a big applause for me?" He asked.

"Everyone knows the Lewis name. Your great-grandfather was a lot more than you thought. But, of course, I couldn't tell you before," Vincent said. Albert nodded, looking around a second before the crowd died down, and the meeting commenced.

Sunshine beamed down through a crack in the tent, hitting him in the eye.

He stood up, feeling his uniform stick to his skin.

"Let's move! Pack it up!" A voice came from outside the tent.

Parks got out of the tent and started packing it up, another soldier walking up to help him get it packed up.

It took them a moment to put the metal rods away, fold the tent, and roll it up onto the side of his pack, but soon, Parks was ready to move out.

"You, hold on. You're private Parks, right?" A voice said behind Parks.

Turning around, he stood at attention as Bullpup approached him.

"Yes, sir!" Parks replied.

"Alright, I need a debriefing. You'll come with my squad back to Tarren's forward operating base. I was told you know one of the Red Hand members who attacked?" Bullpup asked. Parks hesitated.

"Yes, sir. My old boot camp friend, Clay Barrett," Parks said.

"Titan squad was with them? Helping them?" Bullpup asked, taken aback for a moment.

"I believe so, sir. Me and Clay fought for a moment, though he didn't recognize me," Parks replied.

Well, I'll be damned. I thought they were dead. Bullpup thought as he and Parks walked back towards the rest of Parks' squad.

Adam sat at a small table in his room late at night, unable to sleep. He began to think, taking out a pen and a small journal from his shirt pocket.

"August 5, 2020. We're in a new place, with new problems. But despite being in the heart of the former enemy, we're no closer to the truth. We don't know where "The Ark" actually is, nor do we know how far Tarren or Brakata are from here. But what we do know is that if we're ever going to see Tarren soil again, we have to fight. But, that being said, the question arises if we **should** go back. Perhaps one day we'll try to show Tarren that Magic Users aren't a threat, that we are just as human as any of them.

"Sometimes, I ask myself what my purpose is. Why I was taken into Titan Squad, why I let Julie try to help all of those Double Users, and why now am I allowing the people I knew as enemies just days before bring me to a place I've never been and can't even see on a map. But after thinking much about these things, I've come to a conclusion. Myself and Titan Squad were working to destroy our own kind by sending them to the MSF facility in Rotun. If we expose that facility to the public in Tarren, perhaps things can be different. Perhaps the next Chancellor will have a softer outlook on Magic Users? Maybe whatever horrible things are happening to them could sway public opinion?

"I'm not sure. But I know now that it's my purpose to try, and by God, I'm going to try my best to show these people that we're good people and it's the Chancellor that isn't to be trusted. I know what happened when I did,"

Printed in the United States
by Baker & Taylor Publisher Services